NOCTURNES & NIGHTMARES

THE SANDMAN DUET, BOOK ONE

KERI LAKE

For my mom and dad.
Thank you for teaching me the importance of art, for inspiring
me to follow my passions in life, and to never give up.

Love looks not with the eyes, but with the mind, and therefore is winged Cupid painted blind.

— WILLIAM SHAKESPEARE

PROLOGUE

Crouched and hidden behind a rusted burn barrel that was propped against a dilapidated shed, the boy clapped his hands over his ears to block out the screams. There were times when he thought he might've been awake while dreaming, sleepwalking through a nightmare, but he'd never felt cold, or the raising of gooseflesh on his arms, like he did right then. And never in all of his eleven years had he ever seen something so terrifying as what lay on the other side of the shed's door.

The screams grew louder, more intense, as the poor creature begged for its life. A moment ago, when the boy dared a peek through the window, the blood on the floor had looked like a shiny red pool that reflected the fluorescent glow from the lone light flickering over the macabre scene. He'd also seen two misshapen eyes bobbing inside a glass canning jar.

In a brief interlude, when the animal's screeches had died down, murmurs had carried through the tired wooden slats of the door. The sounds of taunting. Letting the boy know his tormentor had caught wind of his hiding place.

"Wake up," the boy whispered to himself. "Please wake up."

Earlier in the day, long before he'd been awakened from sleep by sounds beyond his room, one of the boy's classmates had told him about The Sandman. How he punished those who didn't go to sleep when they were supposed to, by giving them nightmares and, in some cases, stealing their eyeballs to take back to the moon, to feed his children. The boy had laughed it off, thinking it the most ridiculous story that liar had told yet. Not anymore, as the pitch of agonized screams tore through the shed once again, over the whooshing of blood inside his ears.

He wished he'd stayed in his bed, hidden beneath the blankets.

Had he been brave, he would've taken one of the large knives laid out across the floor beside the many tools scattered about. Ones used to inflict the unimaginable pain carried on that hoarse voice bleeding through the wall beside him.

Except, his body wouldn't move. His heart beat so hard against his ribs, he could scarcely breathe.

Monsters are real. He was sure of it. Undeniably certain that the one holding the sharp blade on the other side of the door, his own uncle, was the same man his classmate had told him about.

The figure who lurked in the dark and brought nightmares to life. The one who'd surely find him next, if he made so much as a peep.

The Sandman.

1

NOLA

My heart is an anchor.

The weight of it presses against my rib bones, crushing my insides. Some days it's as light as air, a weightless knot in my chest, begging to be swept away. Today, it's suffocating. Mocking me, as I stare down at the man I hardly know anymore.

A husband on paper, but in reality, he's nothing more than a roommate. The stench of alcohol coming from him is like the cheap perfume of a lover, confessing his affair, and the bottle propped against his chest is the evidence.

I hate that my heart remembers the boy with scruffy blond hair and a skateboard, who called me his baby. I hate that my heart refuses to see the broken mess he's become, the fractured promise of the beautiful life we planned ten years ago.

But that's what love does to the heart. Its gluttony consumes every lie like a sponge, until it becomes heavy and hard, like stone.

I whack my knuckles against Denny's leg. "Wake up."

He doesn't move at first. Not so much as a flinch. I'd

think him dead, if not for the obnoxious snore that tells me otherwise.

"Denny! Wake up!"

At another wallop against his thigh, he snorts and startles awake, as his arms fly out and grip the edges of the couch. "What! Whas goin' on?" He can't even muster an angry groan, or a scowl, with whatever intoxicating dose of alcohol that seems to have rendered his face muscles lax.

Pathetic.

"I need cash. Oliver's birthday is tomorrow."

Huffing, he turns onto his side, burying his face in the couch. "You work."

"Yeah, see ... I used all *my* money on the house payment and utilities. You know, the shit you were supposed to pay me half for?"

"Here comes the ball-busting."

"It's your son's fucking birthday. Surely you can cough up a few bucks for that. I'm assuming, since you had enough for your Jim Beam—"

"Now you're gonna track everything I buy?"

"When you haven't paid me anything in two months? You're damn right I am. I need fifty bucks for Oliver."

"Fifty? What the fuck is fifty bucks?"

"A cake, a toy, and the only thing he asked for, a new coat."

Snorting again, he shakes his head. "I got ten bucks on me." He stuffs his hand into his back pocket and yanks out a ten he lets flutter to the floor."

"You get a couple hundred a week in unemployment, plus cash mowing lawns. Where did all that go?"

"None of your business, that's where."

As anger gets the best of me, I shove at him, jostling his body. "It is my fucking business! If you can't help me with bills, then get out!"

Twisting just enough to peel his face from the couch cushions, he frowns back at me. "'S'at what you want, Nola? Break up our home over money? Said it'd never come to that. Said nothing could ever get in the way of our marriage. Remember?"

"I'm tired of doing everything alone, Denny. The cleaning. The bills. The cooking and the worrying."

His brows wing up with an incredulous smile I'd love to smack right off his face. "Oh, I'm not busting my ass?"

"Are you? I wouldn't know. You haven't given me a dime, except for this measly ten bucks!"

He goes back to cuddling his fifth like a toy he refuses to set down. "I'll get you your damn money. Chill the fuck out." The watch at his wrist catches my eye—a cheap knockoff Rolex that Oliver bought him for Father's Day a couple years back. Surprised he still wears it.

"I want you out of here. Out of my life."

"And then what? You think you'd survive without me? Money aside, you're nothing but a w—"

"Mom?"

I turn to find Oliver standing in the hallway, decked out in his Star Wars jammies, slipping on his thin, black-rimmed glasses.

Head tipped, he glances to Denny and me, no doubt assessing the situation. "What's wrong?"

"It's okay, baby. Go back to bed."

"Can I have a glass of milk?"

"'The hell did your mom tell you—"

"Sure, sweets," I cut Denny short, flipping him off behind my back, where he can see. "I'll bring it to you in a second. Go back to bed, okay?"

Once Oliver is out of sight, I loosen the hundreds of muscles in my face it takes to feign a smile.

"That's why you need fifty bucks. You spoil the little shit."

"That *little shit* hasn't asked for anything any other kid his age would ask for. He deserves all the goddamn presents in the world for having you as a dad." I kick at his feet, taking in a small measure of joy when he recoils.

"Time for another bitch pill, eh, Nola?"

"End of the week. I want you out. And if you don't pay your half of the bills by tomorrow? You can crawl your broke ass out of here the next day. *After* Oliver's birthday."

With a snort, he shakes his head and curls into himself on the couch. "You always were heartless, Nola. This marriage was doomed from the beginning."

My chest throbs in a reminder that I'm not heart*less*. I'm heart*broken*. Not just for me, but for the little boy to whom I'll have to explain everything, every broken piece that's shattered around him, and carefully try to put his world back together.

"I need to run out. I'll give Oliver a glass of milk, and he should go right back to sleep. Think you can handle being an adult for an hour, or two?"

It feels irresponsible leaving Oliver with Denny, but if truth be told, my son is the one most responsible in this scenario. Oliver could practically care for himself, if that were legal.

"Kid's mine, too, in case you forgot."

"Sometimes, I do," I say, swiping up the ten bucks still lying on the floor. Rotten bastard.

In the kitchen, I pour a small bit of milk into a glass, and try not to look at the lump of shit on my couch as I pass him again on the way up the stairs to Oliver's room.

With a smile painted on cold and lying lips, I enter, holding the glass. "Hey, baby. Sorry if Mommy and Daddy were talking too loud. We had some plans to work out for somebody's birthday tomorrow."

That doesn't make him smile. Of course it doesn't. He's too smart for those tricks nowadays.

"Know what I'm getting you?" I set his milk on the nightstand and pull his space-themed blanket up to just below his chin.

"I don't want anything. Except for you and Dad to get along."

"Believe me, Champ. I want that, too."

Crawling into bed beside him, I nudge him over with my hip and slide the blanket to cover my legs. Even at ten years old, he still snuggles up beside me, and I stroke his hair, which smells like oranges. "You're going to have the best birthday ever tomorrow. No fighting. I promise."

"Promise?"

"Promise." Planting a kiss on top of his head, I give him one hard squeeze. "Drink your milk and go to sleep right away, okay?"

"Mom? Do you believe in The Sandman? I mean, he's not real, right?"

"Sandman? Are you asking if I think there's a dude who goes around sprinkling sand in everyone's eyes to put them to sleep?" I frown when he nods, the look of worry etched across his face stirring confusion. Oliver has always been a kid rooted in logic, and it only took him until the ripe age of five to decide Santa, the tooth fairy, and the Easter bunny weren't real. "No. I don't. What's going on with that?"

"Emmett says he's real. He says he watches you every night, waiting for the moment when you're alone and vulnerable. He says he steals your eyeballs. It was in the news, and everything."

"Eyeballs, huh? Emmett drinks too much soda for his

age. If anything, he should be worried about a pissed-off tooth fairy having to collect a mouthful of rotted baby teeth."

"That's gross."

"Indeed. Which reminds me, did you brush your teeth?"

Huffing in obvious frustration, he frowns. "Yes, I did. I'm being serious, Mom. Sometimes, I see … eyes. Watching me through the window at night."

"Well, considering you're on the second floor, a dude would have to be pretty ambitious to climb up to the roof just to spy on a sleeping kid."

"Unless he didn't have to climb."

"C'mon, Oliver. I thought you were too old for that stuff. Too wise. You don't believe in that fantasy stuff, remember?" I push out of his bed and tuck him in, my mind spinning a thousand miles a minute, trying not to let the darkness on the other side of me cast its shadows on him. The unbearable weight of my failed and crumbling marriage that threatens to crush me with such innocent conversation. Sliding his glasses from his eyes, I kiss his forehead and stroke my hand down his cheek. "Time to sleep. Love you, baby."

"Mom?" he says, as I reach for the door. "If The Sandman did exist, though … is he considered good?"

"*Hypothetically*, if there was a dude going around sprinkling sand to make you sleep, I'd like to think he was doing it for the right reasons. The world isn't as crappy as it seems, sometimes, you know?"

"So, even if he does bad things, he's good?"

"Whatever Emmett told you, and I'll be sure to check with his mom on that, it's just a story, Oli."

He drops his gaze from mine and shakes his head. "Please don't talk to his mom. I'll stop asking about it."

"Good. Go to sleep."

"But … do you think Dad is good?"

I press my lips together, to keep the truth from escaping

me and destroying my son's perception of the only man he's ever loved. "I think everyone is born with goodness in them. Some just don't know what to do with it, is all."

Rifling through my jewelry box, I find a simple gold wedding band with a single diamond. Two years ago, I stopped wearing it, and I'm not sure Denny even noticed. My eyes blur with tears as I allow my thoughts to drift to the day Denny proposed to me—probably the worst proposal in the world.

He'd taken me out to an early dinner at some fancy restaurant downtown. We hung out at a bar, watching one of our favorite local bands, then he took me for an evening walk through the park, where I'd first watched him perform tricks on his board. Halfway into the walk, we both started feeling really sick, so we rushed back to his mom's and took turns puking and shitting in the bathroom all night. While pale-faced and camped out beside the toilet, he pulled the ring and proposed.

Wasn't enough that my mom went to her grave hating the guy, but it's as if fate was conspiring against our marriage on top of it all, by giving me the worst case of food poisoning I've ever had.

I slip the ring onto my finger and peek in on Oliver one more time, finding him covered up in his blankets.

Denny's sat up on the couch when I head back down, flipping through channels on the TV, with one hand stuffed inside a bag of Doritos. No doubt, he'll end up passed out on the couch, since the two of us haven't slept in the same bed in months.

"I shouldn't be any longer than an hour. Hour and a half, max. Are you okay to listen for him, or are you too drunk?"

"I'm not drunk. Whatever buzz I might've had, you killed. So, thanks for that."

Asshole.

Sober, Denny could be a decent dad. After all, he's the one who taught Oli to ride a bike and balance on skates before he was old enough to spell his own name. Back when Oliver was a baby, only Denny could calm him when he cried, by plucking his guitar while Oliver dozed off beside him on the couch. Those are the memories that hurt the worst.

The ones involving my son.

Because the thing is, no matter how shitty their parents become, kids still love them.

The changes I plan to make are going to be hard on Oliver, and I don't want to put him through that kind of stress, but I know firsthand how much harder it is to watch at least one parent fall out of love.

It takes closer to two hours to hock my ring for a measly two hundred bucks and drive to the different stores, from where I nab cake supplies and giftwrap and balloons on the way home. When I arrive back, the lights are off inside the two-story house, and Denny's beat-up Honda isn't sitting in the driveway. He's left the curtains open, and I peek into the window to see he's not passed out on the couch as usual, either.

What the hell? Son of a bitch better not have left Oliver alone.

Silence lingers on the air as I enter the dark house, and I dump my bags down on the kitchen counter and race up the stairs.

Oliver's bed is empty.

"If that piece of shit took him to buy more alcohol," I mutter, as I tap the Finder app on my phone. Takes a minute before it zeroes in on his location, and I scowl at the map, giving it a second, because no way in hell would Denny piss me off by taking my son to the shitty side of Chicago. No way in hell.

Not after the hundreds of times I've told him never to take Oliver to hang out with his piece of shit pothead friends on that side of town.

His location doesn't move, though.

In the meantime, and with a small bit of denial, I perform a cursory sweep of the house, then another outside the back door, where the in-law suite behind the house stands equally dark and quiet.

With fury blazing through me, I dial his number on my way back into the kitchen, licking my lips in preparation to cuss him out the moment that bastard answers.

The second the ringing ends and his line connects, I feel a rush of adrenaline pump through me. "You piece of shit! What the hell are you doing? Where the hell are you—"

I trail off when I notice he hasn't said anything. Not even *hello*. I pause to listen for a moment, concentrating on the strange static sound bleeding through the line. Like air being deflated out of a balloon, it squeals, and a wet, barking cough follows.

"Denny?"

A whoosh of air rattles against the earpiece, but in the thick of it, I make out two whispered words: "I'm sorry."

A cold stab of panic pierces my chest. "Denny? What's going on?"

The phone clicks, the abrupt disconnection mirroring the last shred of my calm. With trembling hands, I call again. It rings and rings. In disbelief, I call again.

Still no answer.

I haul ass through the house and out the front door, my hands shaking so bad I can't get the goddamn key lined up in the ignition of my car.

"Fucking come on!"

All I can think about is Oliver. Is he gone? Is he lying somewhere next to his father, dying? Is Denny dying, or is this some sick fucking joke to teach me a lesson for kicking him out?

I speed through streets, desperate to stay focused on that small, vague dot on the map.

As much as I don't want to lose his location, or risk missing another call from Denny, I dial my brother—a detective for the Chicago police department.

In a groggy voice, he answers on the third ring. "Yeah."

"Jonah. It's Nola."

"What's going on? Are you okay?"

"I don't know." Panic wraps itself around my chest, squeezing the breath out of me. "I called … Denny, he … it sounded like he …"

"Slow down."

"I can't." The steering wheel acts as a battering target, against which I slam my hands in frustration. "I can't! I think something happened!"

"Where's Oliver?"

"I think he's with Denny, unless something happened to him. Oh, God, Jonah!"

"Where are you?"

"I'm headed toward West Chicago. Damen Avenue."

"The silos?"

"What do you mean?"

"There's an abandoned grain elevator there. Just …. Just hang tight. I'll check it out."

"No! No. He sounded like … he was … dying. And if Oliver is with him. I need to go."

"Nola, you don't know what you could be walking into. He could've been jumped on that side of town."

"I don't care! My son is with him, Jonah!"

"We're gonna get someone out there now. I'm calling it in now. Just turn around and go back home, and I'll—"

I hang up the phone. I love my brother, but he's a goddamn tool if he thinks I'm going to turn around when my son could be hurt, or worse.

Fuck turning around.

I'm already on the road where the dot on the map tells me Denny's phone is still sitting, on the outskirts of Chicago. Heading south on Damen, I hang a left onto 29th Street, where the dot sits in the center of an abandoned yard. Through the open gates, I pull up alongside Denny's Honda, parked about a hundred yards off from a building covered in graffiti.

What the hell?

The steady drumming against my chest is my heart pounding so fast I can hardly keep up my breathing, as I take in the dark ominous surroundings. A place no mother would ever want her child to venture, for fear of the things that could be lurking within. I want to cry, but I can't. My mind tells my heart to keep its shit together until I find Oliver.

Clambering out the vehicle, I rush toward the Honda and peer in through the windows. Oliver isn't there. From beside the car, its glowing lights the only means of visibility in the encroaching darkness, I scan the abandoned building for an entrance.

That's when I sense something watching me.

Hairs prickle as I turn to see the cup holder of the back-seat propped forward and bright blue eyes peering up at me. I scramble toward them, throwing back the center console of the backseat, and find Oliver curled up in the trunk.

"Baby? Are you okay? Open the latch, Oli."

Even in the dim light of the cabin, I can see him trembling, and my instincts beg me to tear away the damn fabric of the seat to get to him.

13

"Oli! Unlatch the seat!"

A click signals his compliance, and I fold down the seat to see him curled so tight within himself he looks smaller than a ten-year-old. Or perhaps more fragile.

"C'mon, baby. Come out of there." I reach for him, but he shakes his head. "Oli, what happened? Where's your dad?"

His brows dip, eyes brimming with tears, and he shakes his head, but doesn't say a word. Instead, he claps his hands over his ears, and screws his eyes shut.

"Is he inside? In the building?" It occurs to me that Denny could be actively dying somewhere right now. I push to my feet, but my arm is yanked by ice cold hands.

Eyes wide and panicked, Oliver tries to pull me into the car, his effort so ardent, he leaves scratch marks down my skin.

"Hey, hey." Without much choice, I settle next to him and stroke his hair to calm him, while he clings to my arm. "Your dad sounded like he needed help. I just want to check on him." My heart is breaking as I watch the tears slip down his cheeks. A ghost white pallor blanches his usual olive skin tone and he tugs harder and shakes his head.

"Oliver, tell me what happened? Is someone here?"

More tears fill his eyes, and when he nods, my stomach twists at the thought that we're not alone.

"Talk to me. Why won't you talk?"

He ignores me, and though I know it's not out of defiance, the stress is beginning to wear me down, taunting my patience.

"Did you see something?"

His eyes screw tight, his nails digging into my skin, as though my question has planted something horrific inside his mind.

Headlights flash, and on instinct, I duck down, watching

as they flick off, and I can make out my brother's pickup truck idling into the yard.

"Uncle Jonah's here."

A police cruiser trails behind him, and relief washes over me. I tug Oliver over the folded seat and wrap my arms around him, noticing the incessant tremble.

Removing his coat, Jonah approaches the two of us, wrapping Oliver up in a thick wool trench. "Grim and Jeff are going to scope it out. Is he okay?"

I shake my head, letting the first round of tears escape. "He won't say a word."

"Is Denny inside?"

"I think so."

"Anyone else?"

"Yes. I think there is."

The fuzzy interruption of Jonah's walkie-talkie steels my muscles, as I wait to hear an update on Denny.

Jonah steps away from us, and as I lurch forward to follow, fingernails dig into my skin, and Oliver buries his face in my neck.

Brows furrowed, I focus on the murmurings of what little I can hear through that two-way, but one code is unmistakable. It sits heavy on my heart, pulling me under the surface.

The code for murder death kill.

"You're gonna want to come see this." Grim's voice bears the tone of his name. "Oh, God." The gag that follows has my chest feeling numb and cold, and I can barely hang on to Oliver with the weakness settling over me.

"Jonah?" Everything is spinning around me too fast to grasp, and I rest my head against Oliver's, breathing hard through my nose, until it passes and I can set my attention back on my brother. "Jonah?"

Another siren comes with the approach of an ambulance,

blocking out the important pieces of the conversation that have Jonah rubbing his brow and shaking his head.

An irritation that makes me want to run into the building and see for myself.

The contemplation on Jonah's face, when he strides back toward me, says whatever message was relayed is about to change my world. It's like when we were kids and he tried to shield me from the death of our father, taking it upon himself to act as a human tampon for all the scary shit he didn't think I could handle. In turn, he and my mother took the brunt of Gordon Stiever's death, leaving me with little grief to contribute and a lifetime of daddy issues that bled into every relationship after.

"Nola, sit tight for a few minutes. I'm gonna ... check this out."

Still holding Oli, I lurch forward. "Check what out, Jonah? What happened?"

"They found Denny."

"And?"

"Not here, Nola." His eyes fall on Oliver, and it's right then I realize it isn't just my pain he's shielding, but my son's. "I want to check it out, okay?"

"I want to see for myself." The words tumble aimlessly from my lips, because I'm not so sure I want to see what's twisted Jonah's face into tight lines of worry.

"No. Stay with Oliver. He needs you right now."

His words strike me across the face like a slap of reality. Yes, of course. My son needs me. Oliver needs me far more than Denny right now.

My attention shifts to my son, whose once irritating little cowlick reminds me of the one I constantly had to pat down on the top of Denny's head during the better parts of our marriage. One that led to our very first kiss, while sitting on the deck of the half-pipe ramp he built at his mom's.

It somehow fails to register that the caustic conversation we had earlier in the night was our last, aside from his apology. Some small part of me still believes he's alive, and he'll be annoying the shit out of me once everything is settled.

The bigger part of me knows that's a lie.

The heart is an anchor. And mine feels like a stone that's been cast out to the ocean, left to sink into the bottomless darkness.

2

NOLA

Six months later ...

"Tell her I'm a bad mom. Just say it," I whisper, staring through the window of a small conference room.

Inside there, Oliver sits beside a heavyset woman, who's spent months trying to help him find his voice again. A speech therapist, but DeeDee is more than that.

His eyes are on me, angry and resentful for scheduling an appointment two days early. Speech therapy is Friday, but so is the psychotic day of shopping, otherwise known as Black Friday, which means I have to cover a double shift, so here we are. Him hating me and me hating myself.

"I know I'm a shitty mom," I mutter. You don't have to say it."

"You're not a shitty mom." The voice startles me, and I turn just enough to catch Oli's psychologist, Sarah Buckley, standing beside me. "You can't change what happened to him, Nola. And no matter how much you try to blame yourself, it isn't your fault."

"This again, huh?" I snort, returning my attention back

18

to Oli, who won't even try to work with DeeDee. Instead, he looks every bit the rebellious teenager that he isn't yet, with his arms crossed, brow permanently furrowed. Even through the glass that separates us, I can feel the hostility. He's only eleven, but the anger he carries makes him seem so much older. "You know, I think about that night, and the one thing that bothers me most is that I woke Denny up before I left. He'd have probably stayed passed out on the couch while Oli slept, otherwise."

"If you're trying to convince me of something, you're doing a crap job of it." The gentle stroke of her hand down my arm adds just enough contact to spring tears to my eyes. "You were looking for opportunities to make him a better husband and father."

"That's the problem," I say through a blur of tears. "I'm not a quitter. But if I had been …"

"Oliver is still here, Nola. Focus on that and quit beating yourself up for things you can't go back and change."

"I'm sorry. You're not my therapist. That's not fair."

"Doesn't stop me from caring." Her arm nudges mine, and I offer a smile. "How's the pottery going?"

"Haven't really done a whole lot of it in the last few months. Picking up shifts leaves me exhausted most nights."

"You're a hard-working mom. Remember to take time for yourself." She crosses her arms. "Take a bath, read a book. Whatever you have to do to unplug and *enjoy* that time without the guilt. It's good for Oliver to understand that, as well."

"He hates me. He knows Denny and I were … that our marriage was …. I still resent him, even after death. Every time I have a moment where I think I could forgive him, I remember that he took my son to meet with a drug dealer in an abandoned building. He endangered his life, and for what? A fix?"

"And how do you think a mother *should* react to that?"

Doctor Buckly has a knack for trying to lessen my guilt, but she's not been successful at eliminating it altogether.

"I just want to do right by my son. I want him to feel safe again. To trust the world again."

"Then, keep doing what you're doing. Give him time to mourn and heal. And give yourself time to do the same. Your guilt is getting in the way of what your soul needs right now."

"My soul?" I want to laugh at that. I don't even know if I still have one, it's been so long since I felt anything. "No. I don't cry for him anymore. Surely, someone who loved the other person would need more than six months to get over it."

"We all mourn in our own ways. And you're clearly not over it. How are you sleeping at night?"

Rolling my head against my shoulders fails to loosen the incessant knot of remorse for having brought all this up. "Like I said, Sarah. You're not my therapist. You don't have to do this."

"Nola. How are you sleeping?"

"Couple hours. It's the same every night. Sometimes, Oli wakes up screaming. Sometimes, I *swear* he wakes up screaming." Two months ago, I started sleeping with a knife under my pillow, but I don't tell her that, because only crazy, paranoid women sleep with weapons.

"If you'd like, I can refer you to a friend of mine. She's a psychiatrist. She can prescribe something for—"

"No. No pills. I don't need to be hopped up on prescription drugs all night. I lived with that as a teenager. I know how it feels when your mom is practically comatose."

I wish I could say Denny's was the only tragedy I've been through, but my life is a circle, and outside of the lines is a darkness that wants in so badly, it pokes at me every day. It poked at my mother, until she finally gave in and let it consume her entirely.

The fringes weren't always so bleak, though. In fact, there was a time they were so bright, we couldn't see past the blinding light. That was before my older sister disappeared. I was only ten, on the brink of eleven at the time—about the same age as Oliver. She left for a date with a boy I'd never met and didn't come home. Ever. The questions she left behind morphed into a vacuous hole that's never gone away. So I'm no stranger to tragedy, or the effect of mind-numbing drugs meant to soften the lines, to coexist with that darkness. I don't want a single drop of it inside me.

"It doesn't do Oli any good, if you're running on fumes, either."

"Lesser of two evils, as far as I'm concerned." I am tired. Tired and frustrated with how difficult it is just getting out of bed every morning. Maybe Denny was right when he said I'd never make it without him. Maybe part of me died alongside him that night, and this is my hell.

I stare back at my son, who sits with his head in his palms, his frustration clear as he kicks at the legs of the table in a poor attempt to calm an oncoming tantrum. "Just tell me this much, Sarah. Will he ever forgive me?"

"For what?"

"For lying to him. For telling him monsters didn't exist."

I turn the car into the McDonald's drive thru and order a chocolate milkshake and fries, just like every Friday after one of Oli's sessions. Today, he doesn't eat much, but picks at the small pack of fries like a bird, while we drive toward Jonah's house. My brother's wife, Diane, usually picks Oli up from the house after school for me, and takes him until I get home from my night shift at the diner, but as I have to work on Thanksgiving and the day after, they'll be taking him until Sunday. Doesn't help that Denny didn't have a life insurance policy, so I try to grab as many hours as I can.

It's been a while since I've left Oliver alone overnight, and I'm, admittedly, nervous about it.

"Hey, you won't even miss me." A fake chuckle escapes my lips, in a poor effort to hold back tears.

Oliver tosses his fries toward the cup holder between us, which sends a few of them bouncing onto the floor.

"Don't be like that. Look, I know it's hard right now, but … it's going to get better. I promise. Just stick with me, okay, kiddo?" Tears blur my view, and I clear my throat. "I can't do this without you."

Despite his head being turned toward the window, I can see the scowl on his face, the permanent marks of his resentment that have added new lines.

"I was thinking maybe … in a few weeks, I'll take a few days off, and we can go up to grandpa's cabin. Do some fishing. I'll let you bait the hook." This time my chuckle is real and brimming with tears. "That sound good to you?"

His chest rises and falls with a huff, and he turns back toward the windshield. Without looking at me, he nods and nabs a fry from beside us.

A few days off will be tight, but if it brings him back to me, I'm willing to figure shit out with the bills. As if I need another reason to hate Denny, I wouldn't owe anything more than taxes on the house if we hadn't taken out a loan against it to pay off his debts and tools that were meant to start a new business and change our lives. My father left the house to me when he died, and Jonah inherited the cabin. Between waitressing and the small craft shows where I sell my hand-thrown pottery, I'm still not making it.

I pull up to the curb of my brother's house, where Diane

stands on the front porch. Looking far more healthy and beautiful than I feel right now, in her black turtle neck and hoop earrings, she waves, her face plastered with a bright smile, and makes her way toward the car. Unable to have children of her own, she's practically begged to have Oliver over to stay with them, and as much as I should be comforted by the love and joy she gets from spending quality time with my son, I'm green with jealousy about it.

But I do appreciate her.

Young and vibrant, she's a reminder of everything I used to be, when Denny and I were first married. Sometimes, I wonder if I'm just as much a reminder to her of what happens when you reach the end of that happy road.

"Hey, Potterhead! Ready for a movie marathon?" she asks, as she reaches the passenger door.

The question catches me off guard. Six months ago, that was a favorite past time with my son, and now he has no interest in watching anything with me. "You guys are watching *Harry Potter*? I didn't .... I mean ... that's awesome."

The door clicks as Oliver nabs his duffle bag from the floor, and I reach out for his arm. "Wait. No kiss?"

He leans toward me and lays a quick peck on my cheek, before slipping out through the half opened passenger door and up the staircase to the house.

Diane's gaze trails after him a moment, before she swings her attention back to me. "Hey, Nola ... if I overstepped—"

"You didn't. At all. We haven't watched those movies in ... months." I've tried to engage Oliver in doing the things we used to love before that night, but everything I've tried is a reminder of everything that's different now.

Diane stuffs a hand inside her pocket and pulls out an envelope with a bank emblem on it.

Shaking my head, I set the gearshift to drive, but not

before she reaches inside and drops the envelope on the passenger seat, where a stack of twenties spills out.

"Take it. Your brother wanted you to have it, but he knew you'd refuse him. I'm not so nice. You need it, Nola."

"I'm not ... taking money from you."

"I'm not taking it back."

In spite of the tears in my eyes, a laugh escapes me. "You already do so much for me, Diane. I can't take this from you."

"Watching Oliver helps me cope. So there's that." She turns away, and I can see *her* eyes are filled with tears, too. For three years, she's tried to have a baby with my brother. Every month, she's greeted with the disappointment of loss. Oliver's acted as a substitute child, until the surrogate mother they've hired delivers, which should be sometime around Christmas. "You don't let people do enough for you. Go ... buy something nice for yourself, and for Oliver. And try not to worry so much about things, okay? Jonah and I ... we got you."

"I know." Jesus, the more she talks, the more tears I have to wipe away. "Thank you for everything." Sniffling, I clear my throat and curl my knuckles around the steering wheel. "I'm actually thinking about renting out the in-law suite in the back." It's not something I want to do, since I've grown just as wary of the world as Oliver, but a few extra bucks a month will certainly ease things, particularly with Christmas right around the corner.

"Be sure to have Jonah run a background check on whoever decides to take it. Don't want some weirdo moving in."

I snort at that, shaking my head. "I've had enough of those. Believe me. Bethany's husband asked me if I'd consider a threesome with the two."

A burst of laughter flies from Diane's mouth, quickly capped behind her hand. "Are you kidding me?"

Bethany works with me at the diner, and it's common knowledge that she and her husband swing. In fact, the owner has had to pull her aside to keep her from propositioning the customers. That didn't stop her husband the last time he came in, though.

"I wish. I'd masturbate a cucumber before I'd crawl into bed with those two."

"Hey, don't knock it 'til you try it, sister." The waggling of her brows sets my teeth on edge, and I have to mentally force myself not to grimace at the thought of her and a cucumber when my brother isn't around. "Just make sure you grab some lube."

"Okay, TMI." Eyes clamped shut, I pretend to bang my head against the steering wheel. "I gotta get to work. Thank you ... for Oliver, for the cash ... for the lube advice."

"Don't fear the lube. Pour a glass of wine, put on some music, and ..."

"Yeah. Let's not go there. Let Oli know I'll miss him, okay? And I love him."

"I will. Love you."

"Love you back."

3

VOSS

Apathy is a man's most destructive weapon.

Drawn, agonizing moans echo through the dark room, which is lit only by the naked bulb dangling overhead. It's been hours since I've last taken a piss, and at the moment, that's the only thing consuming my thoughts. Not the middle-aged man whose life is slowly seeping out of the wounds I poked into his body, or the fact that I'm about to add another soul to my morbid collection. No, I'm thinking about the thirty-two-ounce coffee I downed before dragging this poor sap's ass into the interrogation room about six hours ago, which has gone it's rounds through my body and is just as ready as I am to make an exit.

"Who made the deal?" The calm in my voice comes as a comfort to some, unless they're laid out like Tony here, staring up at me as if he's reached the end of his wick.

"I ..." His answer is cut short by a gurgling cough, and a glob of blood smacks his cheek, small bits of his insides springing forth and sliding down his skin. "Told you."

'Fuck sakes, man. I'm about to piss all over this stubborn prick.

Wouldn't be so bad if a perfect record of extraction wasn't on the line. I never fail my clients, and if Tony has to be ground into hamburger before he realizes that, then I guess I'll ignore the urges begging me to add a golden shower to his list of tortures. Hands braced on the edge of the table, I shake my head and expel an exasperated huff.

I'm tired. He's undoubtedly tired. This has to be the most tenacious subject I've had in years. Bordering on ridiculous at this point. The guy's already lost an ear, six of his ten fingers, a kneecap, and about four liters of blood from the looks of it. I can't even begin to imagine what's holding him together, besides some ungodly will to remain silent.

I turn to the tray of tools beside me and lift a scalpel, twisting it in front of him. "Do you know how many muscles hold the eyeball in place, Tony?"

His bottom lip curves with his quiet, tearless sobbing. Bastard must be weak as hell, if he can't even muster a convincing cry.

"Six. Six muscles and an optic nerve. Enucleation is the detachment of those muscles and that nerve from the eyeball, and I'm not going to lie to you, Tony. Cutting an eyeball out isn't like cutting off your ear. You *may* experience some discomfort in this, as I have to tug at the eyeball itself, once it's popped, in order to keep those muscles nice and taut for the blade." I rub a gloved thumb across his brow, and he flinches at my touch, his whimper the only sound he's made consistently through this dog and pony show. "But these orbital bones make it tolerable to lose an eye. Not like … say, I removed your kidney." I set the blade to the side, staring down at the shit brown irises I may have to stab out of his skull before I get to take that piss. "Or we can say to hell with all that, and you can just tell me, honestly this time, who made the deal."

Snot mixed with blood bubbles from his nose, as his face

pinches into another sob, and he rolls his head on the table. "I don't—"

"Don't tell me you don't know. I'll rip your goddamn eyeballs out with my fingers, if you tell me you don't know. I don't even care about precision at this point."

My phone buzzes beside me, and Milo's name pops up on the screen. I don't typically answer calls during a session, but this guy has tested my patience, and I can't exactly ignore a call from the boss. Most guys in the agency have never heard the top dog's voice, let alone have him on speed dial. With my wrist, I awkwardly slide my arm across the screen.

Doesn't answer the call.

Groaning, I remove my glove, dropping it on Tony's face and answer the call on speakerphone.

"Yeah."

"You're in a session?"

"I am." I slide the glove from his face and offer Tony a smile and a wink, as he continues to whimper and roll his head. The pallor of his skin tells me the guy isn't going to last much longer, so Milo better get on with his interruption, or I'll be reporting back my first failed extraction.

Something I refuse to do.

"Voss ... we got the wrong guy."

His words send a zap of electricity down my spine.

"I'm sorry, there's a ... shitty echo in this basement. Sounded like you said we have the wrong guy, or something. Hang on." I swipe up the phone from the tray, gritting my teeth to keep from inadvertently stabbing another hole in Tony.

"Jackson pulled the wrong profile. The guy you have should've gone to Carter."

Carter is another agent of The Gallows who covers the Meatpacking District. And Jackson is the halfwit internist, almost like a paralegal for the morally suspicious, who has officially landed my shit-list now.

Christ, no wonder Tony kept throwing out names for the DeLuca family. Here, I thought he was just being a patronizing dick. Bastard probably had no idea who, or what, I've been talking about the last six hours.

A whoosh of breath crackles down the line as Milo huffs. "My apologies. This is a goddamn fiasco."

"A fiasco? No. A fiasco is when you order a fucking caramel latte, and the asshole barista gives you a caramel macchiato instead. A fiasco is when the surgeon removes the wrong kidney, and you end up a millionaire with a free kidney transplant."

"Voss. We'll make this right. I promise you. I'll, uh … report back to …" He clears his throat and coughs. "*Richard* with an update."

Eyes clamped shut, I mentally count back from ten, like a therapist once told me to do before I slammed her against the wall and fucked her brains out, instead. Didn't work for me then, and it sure as hell isn't working for me now.

"Rajna can finish the job. He's on his way there now."

I glance back at *the job*, lying sprawled out on the table, dead as the doornails I drove into his shins. "Tell him not to bother," I say, clicking off the call and tossing the phone onto the tray that jingles the tools there. Not so much as a flinch from Tony. Tucking two fingers against his neck, I feel for the pulse I know isn't there. Deadened eyes and gaping blue lips already provided the visual confirmation of that. "Fuck."

It's not so much the mistake itself that bothers me. Not like we're killing saints in this line of work. It's the lack of professionalism that pisses me off. The absolute disregard for it since Kelch, my mentor, kicked the bucket, leaving his shithead nephew, *Richard*, in charge of operations. Not even

Milo can say the kid's name without clearing his throat and emphasizing it every damn time. Must be hard for a retired Special Forces soldier, with as many combat tours as he's done, to take orders from some spineless twit who just happens to have the connections to keep the business going. Nearly fifty agents work for The Gallows, spanning across the globe—all of us former military, or some line of work that's allowed us to become highly effective at killing without conscience.

All of us under the direction of a man who prefers to be called Dick.

Blood drips over the edge of the table as I gather up my tools and stuff them into the autoclave bag. A cleaner for The Gallows will ensure there isn't a speck of evidence remaining, though I'm often tempted to hide some shit, just to make Milo's asshole pucker.

A damn shame. I shake my head, sealing the autoclave bag, and stare down at the dead guy as I remove my gloves . Killing for purpose is one thing. Killing the wrong guy for purpose just pisses me off. Which means Jackson's in deep shit the next time I see him.

A worn brick building looks like any other off Church street, with its sealed brown doors set below the fire escape. Having already scanned my surroundings, I type the code on the keypad that's hidden beneath what looks like a line of mailboxes, and slip my key in the lock to enter.

The guts of the place are nothing like the outside. All state-of-the art technology that encapsulates the modern décor. Any passerby would mistake the joint for an abandoned shithole, but if they tried to break in, they'd find themselves trapped in something of an escape room, rigged with a number of fun little games I can control from my phone. Cost me a bit of money, but as a bachelor in New York who nets more in a single job than most people earn as an annual salary, it's the fun things that make it all worthwhile.

After tossing my cufflinks and watch onto the granite countertop, I make my way to the fridge and nab a bottle of beer. Bourbon is my drink of choice, but I need something cold to douse the rage burning through me since I left the job.

When The Gallows was first established about ten years back, we were given a file with a name, and it was our job to track, target and capture. These days, there are assistants, like fucking paralegals, assassins in training, who gather the intel on a subject, so all we have to do is show up with a smile. Lazy ass lions in a cage getting fed steaks on a platter.

No chase. No purpose. Nothing but a witless kill.

Kicking back a drink, I feel my phone buzz inside my pocket, and pull it out to see Milo's number flashing across the screen.

"What's going on, Milo?" I answer.

"About today ... don't let one mistake—"

"Look, I'm going to level with you. You've been a great mentor and friend, but this shit's getting old. And I'm not just talking about Jackson's fuck-up. There's nothing in it for me, anymore. Thrill is gone, man."

"Voss. You're our best agent. I know this place has turned into a goddamn media franchise since Kelch, but don't go fucking existential on me. You've got a bright future ahead of you."

A bright future in what, exactly? Poking holes into various organs? Perhaps I'll strive to become a professional kneecap buster?

"Take a break for a couple months. Check out a tropical

island, order some fruity drinks and fuck some exotic ass. Whatever you gotta do to reset your brain. Guaranteed, you'll be ready to get back to the grind afterward."

Rubbing my hand across my face, I shake my head, because I already know a tropical island and some exotic ass isn't going make this shit any more appealing. "We'll see, Milo."

"I'll call you in a few weeks."

Clicking off the phone, I tip back the bottle and head toward my bedroom. "Lights on," I command, and a soft ambient glow fills the room like the sun rising up. "Heat shower."

Seconds later, the soft patter of the shower echoes from the adjacent bathroom, and I peel my white shirt from my shoulders. It's then I remember the blade I had to disarm when I first encountered Tony—even that felt like an inconvenience, the way things run these days. He managed to slice across a skull tattoo on my bicep, another scar to add to my growing collection.

The worst one stretches temple to cheek, outside of my eye, and serves as a reminder that no one, not even Milo, for whom I might be willing to take a bullet, can be entirely trusted.

I finish undressing and shower quickly, letting the unforgiving heat of the water wash away the day's frustrations. Towel wrapped at my bottom half, I exit the bathroom, running my hand through damp short-cropped hair, as I come to a stop in front of a wall. "Panic room open."

"Password" the robotic voice asks.

"Fuck me."

The wall clicks and slides to the right, revealing a dark staircase that self-lights as I step down onto the concrete in bare feet. The wall slides closed behind me and clicks locked while I descend, more lights ahead flicking on with every step.

Down there, a cocktail bar stands across from a king-sized bed, and beside it, a Saint Andrews cross is flush against the wall. A shelf stocked with food, and bottles of premium water and liquor means I could essentially survive inside this chamber for months, if I desired.

Some days, I think I could. Particularly as this place was designed for my favorite pastime.

A cage against one wall holds a woman, naked and pale, curled into a ball. Her arms are bound by leather cuffs, loose enough she can slide them off, if she wants, but she won't. Just like she won't remove the blindfold over her eyes, or the stilettos strapped to delicate feet.

She won't because she knows it'll exacerbate my frustration if she does, and there's nothing she wants more in this world than to please me. Because pleasing me means pleasure for her, the kind that transcends the mind into subspace.

Unfortunately, her reward will have to wait another night.

I unlock the cage, allowing her to crawl out on all fours.

"Please, let me go," she bleats, and scuttles to get away from me.

Gripping one of her ankles, I drag her back toward me, which sets off a last ditch effort to get loose. Heels peck against my arm, as she kicks and claws at the floor, the sight of her struggle working its magic on my cock.

"Yeah, that's it." I grit through clenched teeth, yanking her backward, and grab her by the mid-section.

She wriggles against my body, knocking the towel away, and I slam her against the top of the cage, my chest to her back, as I draw her hair out of my face. "Please. I want to go home."

Even in three-inch heels, she doesn't quite meet my height, but it's enough that, when bent forward over red velvet padding that cushions her breasts, her ass sits propped high enough to meet my cock.

"This is your home for as long as I say."

She's clean and sterile—two things I specifically requested when I placed the order for her a couple weeks back.

Squirming, she fights me, as I gather her arms and hold her down.

"No! Stop! Stop!"

And I would, but that's not her safe word. It's one of the acceptable forms of resistance that we both agreed on, mostly because it gets me excited.

Except tonight, I feel like I'm merely going through motions, and the fact that this is all staged isn't doing much to help that.

I'd hoped for a quick fuck before bed, but my dick is getting increasingly flaccid by the second. Staring down at her ass, I spread her apart, confirming she hasn't removed the plug I inserted within hours of her arrival. Below it, her pussy glistens, telling me she's already wet and ready.

Steak for the lions.

She doesn't talk, or mutter a word, unless in struggle, because she isn't supposed to. I don't care to know anything about her, or what she likes. In exchange, she'll walk out of here with enough money to support whatever endeavors she chooses. Most of the girls I've ordered are in college, looking to finance a career, but that's information volunteered by the organization that provides them, not because I bothered to ask.

I line myself at her entrance and rub my hand across my jaw, already bored with this. Sex has become as dull as killing. As menial a task as brushing my teeth and checking my messages later.

I try to follow a rule that if I'm not feeling it, there's no sense beating a dead horse, but I know a quick fuck would set me right again. If I could get hard and come.

I feel nothing.

She's mine for one more week, but from the looks of it, I don't think I'll be keeping her for one more day.

It's not her fault, but mine.

With a shake of my head, I don't even bother to enter her, and instead, step back. I notice the slickness dripping down the back of her thighs and nab my towel to wipe away the evidence of her excitement, which at this point is nothing more than a slap in the face. Fastened with a loose knot, the blindfold slides easily over her head. "Gather your things. I'll be returning you first thing in the morning."

She pushes off the cage and stares down at me, brows winged as if she might cry.

"You did nothing wrong. I'll provide full payment for your services."

"Master Voss, I—"

"You don't have to call me Master. You're welcome to sleep in the bed tonight. Or, if you'd like, I can call an Uber to pick you up once you're packed."

"Are you sure I didn't do anything wrong? I didn't use the safe word once this time."

"Positive." I nod my head toward the door at the opposite side of the room. "Through that door is an exit to Reade Street. The code to get out is HELP. Make sure you have all your things, as you can't get back in once you leave."

"And if I don't want to leave?" she asks meekly, lowering her gaze from mine. "I mean, if I decide to stay the night?"

"Then, make sure you have all your things in the morning when you leave. There's a phone and credit card in the nightstand should you wish to call a ride. Please don't steal the phone. It's a pain the ass to replace, and the credit card is nothing more than a prepaid, so you won't get much from it."

"So, I guess this is goodbye." At my silent stare, she lowers her gaze toward her hands. "Thank you for an ... intense week. Probably the scariest and most exciting I've had in a long time."

I wish I could say the same. In fact, I wish I could've blown one last load before setting her free, but life is too short to waste on someone so eager and willing to please. I don't want a silver platter. I want the chase. The target and capture, and to get hard from the mere thought of conquer. I want fight and resistance, and all the things for which I've deprived myself the last decade.

"I'll forward payment immediately. Goodnight," I say, turning away from her.

Up the staircase and through the door that locks behind me, I make my way back to the kitchen, where I down a shot of bourbon, then head to my office.

On the desk sits an old wooden metronome, with a pendulum that I release as I pass by. The incessant *click, click, click* beats against the tension in my muscles, and I slump into the leather, office chair in front of the window facing Church Street, letting the sound calm me. Staring off takes me back to the days when my mother played piano, those brief and blissful moments encapsulated in seventy beats per minute, before my grandfather came home and tainted the mood with his overbearing temper. As a child, I suffered from terrible headaches, the kind that left me clutching my skull on the floor with tears in my eyes, and in her effort to soothe the pain, she would often play something soft and quiet. I loved watching her play, while those ticks matched the natural rhythm of my heart.

Only seconds later, I feel the warmth of the bourbon and the ease of my muscles slipping into a more relaxed state.

My phone blinks with a new message. I open it to an email from my CryptMail account. It's an encrypted email, evident in the string of numbers of my address that keeps it anonymous. I created the account back when I lived in Chicago and advertised on Tor as a hitman for hire. Haven't been active on the site in nearly a decade, and I can't begin to imagine how someone might've stumbled upon it after all these years.

The message reads: *Want to play a game?*

"These motherfuckers," I mutter, shaking my head. With a huff, I click reply and type: *Sure. Solitaire? Go fuck yourself.*

No sooner do I set my phone down than the damn thing chimes with another message. Asshole must be at his computer waiting for my response.

For kicks, I open it.

I need you to fix a problem for me.

I don't fix other people's problems anymore, I type back.

The mailbox blinks a new message. Twitchy must have his fingers hovering over the keyboard, for chrissakes.

Are you familiar with the The Sandman of Chicago?

What is that, like a musical? *Nope*, I reply.

Perhaps the name Carl Jenson rings a bell?

Blood cold as ice, I stare down at the name. Of course it rings a bell. A loud, blaring obnoxious bell that I silenced nearly two decades ago, to the date, when I pushed him off the old bridge behind my grandfather's estate—the most unsatisfying death I ever witnessed.

Who is this?

Our conversation becomes more of a chat, as he continues to respond within seconds. *He's found a new toy. Pretty thing with pretty brown eyes.*

Becoming a hitman wasn't entirely by chance, and neither was my innate proclivity for sadism. I learned from the best, the twisted thrill of watching things die running through my veins since I was a boy. Carl Jenson was, by far, the most sadistic psychopath I ever met, which is saying a lot coming from a man who works for an agency that tortures high profile criminals. He was also the uncle I got stuck with after my mother died.

Where?

Your old stomping grounds, of course.

As tempting as all of this may be, I'm not interested in returning to the shithole neighborhood where I grew up. *Carl Jenson is dead.*

Perhaps. But if you're wrong, then brown eyes will make a stunning addition to my collection. I'm prepared to wire twenty thousand in Bitcoins to the address indicated on your website.

For what?

To find me. A fun little game of cat and mouse.

I don't play games. And neither should you.

You used to enjoy the games we played. Don't you remember?

Pain throbs in my skull as I grind my teeth, my thoughts carrying me back to twenty years ago, when I was at the mercy of my sadistic bastard of an uncle, who enjoyed tormenting me for fun.

I killed him myself. Watched his body carried off by the river's rapid current. To hell with this asshole. For a split second, I wonder if it's Jackson, messing with me, but no way he'd risk my retaliation after what happened this afternoon.

Fuck your games. Carl is dead. Let it go.

I click out, just as a new message comes in. This one with an attachment. Must be the bourbon that makes me click it open. The attached news article is a story about a serial killer in the Chicago area, known locally as The Sandman. As I read on, one particular detail sends a cold chill up my spine: he cuts his victims eyeballs out and fills the sockets with sand made of bone meal.

My thoughts drift back to my childhood, to the many

carcasses of animals my uncle captured and tortured, and left scattered around my grandfather's property. In all cases, their eyes had been removed and filled with sand made of bone meal.

Who is this? I type back, the possibility becoming more real.

You have three weeks. Her name is Nola Tensley.

Why would he tell me her name? That makes no sense.

Who is she to you?

I wait for his response, but nothing more arrives. Tipping back another sip of bourbon, I stare down at the thread of messages spanning the length of my phone screen.

Impossible. I watched him hit the water. I watched his body crumple with the impact and sink below the surface with the racing current. I had no doubts at the time that he was dead, and after nearly two decades of peace and quiet, I'd be hard pressed to believe otherwise.

If, by some small measure of chance, he is alive, though, the trip would be well worth it. As much as I'd like to believe my intentions are saving some unsuspecting victim from becoming his next sand-bagged corpse, the good guy shit was never really my thing.

No, the worm on the hook for me is Carl, whose face I see in every bastard that lands beneath my blade, and every time someone touches my face, I'm reminded of that night.

I've dreamed of the day I could repay the favor of destroying his life, slow and meticulously, just as he did mine. The excitement stirring in my blood tells me that walking away from this isn't going to be an option for me. The timing is a little uncanny, freakish even, but I can't deny that fate sure as hell picked the right moment to drop this little crap-cannon into my lap. And my mind's already ahead of me. Already planning.

Hotels and motels will be too easy for him to track me

down, even with cash, and I don't need some nosy maid rifling through my shit, so I'll need to find a place to lay low.

A place I can keep a close watch on this Nola Tensley.

4

NOLA

It's after three when the diner starts to settle after the lunch rush. The balls of my feet ache, my shoulders feel like twenty pound weights are slung over them, and I've got a headache from hell. Didn't get much sleep again the night before. Even with Oliver out of the house, I woke up to his screams, only to find his bed was completely empty —as it should've been. But that didn't stop me from freaking out at first, when I jumped out of bed half asleep.

Stealing a quick break, I head out the back door of the diner, to check my phone and have a much-needed cigarette. I don't smoke as a general rule, but I like having a pack on hand while at work. Sometimes, it's nice to sneak away.

There's a notification up on my screen from an unknown number. Could be a bill collector, or some shit spam call. Or a response to the ad I placed for a renter.

When it pops up again, in real time, I answer, "Hello?"

"I understand you have an apartment for rent?" The voice on the other end catches me off guard. Deep and rich, undeniably masculine, it practically vibrates through the phone.

"Uh … yes. I do." I catch myself, remembering I decided

41

not to rent to a guy. Nothing against guys in general, but I don't want to end up in a situation with a creeper. "I'm sorry, it's … only for a month," I say, hoping it's enough to make him lose interest.

"Perfect. I'll take it."

"Well … you … um. It's twelve hundred dollars for the month. With a deposit. Paid up front." I'm throwing out a ridiculous deal to this guy, and as soon as he finds out it's nothing but a small four hundred square foot studio, he's going to tell me to go to hell.

"I can do that."

"It's not really an apartment. More like one big divided room. Quite small, actually. And it's not really convenient, or close to downtown."

"It's fully furnished?"

"With outdated furniture, yes."

"If I didn't know better, I'd say you weren't interested in renting to a man."

"What? No! Oh, my God, that's …" *Not a lie.* "So far from the truth. I'm just … being totally honest with you."

"I appreciate it. I'll drop by the deposit and sign whatever paperwork you need."

Whoa, whoa, whoa. I don't know who this guy thinks he's talking to, but I'm not about to rent to the first asshole that calls my number.

"I'll need to do a background check?" *Really, Nola? Are you sure you need to do a background check?*

"Of course. I can provide whatever you need. I'd like to move in this evening."

"This … wait, wait. This is moving …. I just need to process this a second." I slap a hand to my forehead, trying to make sense of what's going on. I'd planned to rent the place, *hoping* for five hundred a month, realizing most would probably take one look at the place and insist on four. This guy is willing to pay *twelve*, and he hasn't even seen it. Surely, when he sees it, after agreeing to pay such an ungodly amount over the phone, he'll want to strangle me. *I'd* want to strangle me.

"Sure. Process away."

"We'll start with a background check first. If you could …"

"Do you have a pen? I'm happy to provide my name and social security."

Again, I'm slapped upside the head. Who the hell gives out that information over the phone? "Just like that? You don't even know me. I mean, I could be some weirdo, roping in unsuspecting guys. A grifter. Or a black widow."

"A grifter? I never thought of that. Or a black widow, for that matter." The amusement in his voice adds an interesting spin to his response. "How about if I come by and see it. Make sure you're not trying to lure me into a web."

"When?"

"Tonight. Eight o'clock."

"Eight? That's …" Dark, and the perfect cover for bad shit to go down. "How about tomorrow morning? Not too early. I'm working a double tonight."

"How's ten?"

"Ten works." I don't even really know what I'm agreeing to. Not even posted a full forty-eight hours, I've already got a potential renter who's willing to pay more than double what I planned to rent it for. I should feel guilty about that, but if this guy turns out to be a creep, I'll consider the extra seven hundred an added security deposit—as in, the cost of adding cameras, and shit, to my house.

I click off the call and head back inside, still somewhat stunned.

Bethany's fixing her lipstick at the lunch counter, and I approach from behind and knock her elbow, sending a line of candy apple red up to her nose.

"Bitch!" she says, chuckling when she wipes the mess with a napkin.

"Sorry. Couldn't help myself."

"You're in a good mood. What's that about?"

"I think I have someone to rent the in-law suite. Means I don't have to take all these extra shifts. For the next month, anyway, unless he decides to rent longer."

"*He?*"

Ugh, anything with a dick, and she's all over it. "We'll see. If he turns out to be a creeper, I'll be sure to send him to you and Harv."

"You met him yet?"

"No. Not yet. Supposed to check out the apartment tomorrow morning."

"What if he's tall and muscular? And hot as hell?"

"I'm not looking for a hookup, Beth. I just need some extra cash for Christmas."

"Hookups are good for you. A healthy sex life is important, and let's face it, you didn't have much of that when Denny was alive."

I don't answer that, because she's right. Denny and I shared the occasional quickie in the bathroom, while Oliver was asleep, mostly just to blow off some of the tension between us. Always felt like more of a weekly quota than a sex life.

"Well, that's what vibrators are for, right?"

"If you use them, yes. You're not still carrying the torch for him, are you? He was never good enough for you."

My brows furrow. "I don't carry any torches. For anyone. I'm just not out to screw the first thing that walks through the door."

No sooner do the words spill from my mouth than the bell rings, signaling a new customer. Simon Jeffries takes his usual seat toward the back of the diner, wearing the bright, familiar smile the other waitresses have come to adore. He's in his early twenties, not married, no kids from what we've gathered, and tips better than any other customer who comes in as regularly as he does.

Every afternoon at 1:45pm, to be exact.

A fairly shy guy who loves talking about technology and robotics, all the shit I don't care to talk about.

"Dibs on Simon!" Bethany shuffles toward his table, drawing a pad and pen from her apron.

Once settled, Simon flashes Bethany a crooked set of teeth while he cleans his silverware with a napkin. She falls into the booth across from him, leaning forward as though the two are conversing instead of placing an order for food.

Rolling my eyes, I nab a cloth and wipe down the counter. At the chime of the bell, I glance up to see Harv, Bethany's husband, striding toward me.

"Oh, Christ," I mutter, looking for a place to hide, but it's too late. The bastard already has his sights set on me.

"How's it going, Nolick." He comes in every day to take Beth out to his van for lunch. I'm guessing they screw while they're out there, since he tends to park toward the back of the lot, but I've never cared to prove that point.

"It's Nola. You know it's Nola. Quit being a dick."

"Given any thought to my proposition?"

"You're actually not supposed to be propositioning me. Dale said if he catches you, he's going to throw you onto a fryer."

"Dale's dramatic. Went to school with the little prick. And I do mean *little prick.*"

"Well, I'm working—you know, like a real job—so I'm going to cut this convo short." I turn to walk away and feel a tight grip of my arm. The moment I spin around, he lets me go, likely seeing the potential for murder in my eyes.

"Nola, I'm begging you. *Begging.* Just one night. I

promise I'll be gentle." He leans in with a smile that's missing an eyetooth. "You know how couples have their free passes, right?"

"You guys swing. I don't think that applies to you."

"So, like, I asked Beth, who's the one person in the whole wide world she'd want to fuck freely. Like, whenever she wants. Like, I'd share her with this dude, right? She picks Tom Hardy. Pfft! Tom Hardy." He shakes his head and glances over his shoulder toward where she's still sitting with Simon.

"And?"

He swings his attention back to me, not that I want his attention, but I feel compelled to support that *I'd* fuck Tom Hardy, and I'm not even interested in sex.

"And … I picked you. Like, you could move in with us, and shit. Not that you'd want to, but you're *my* Tom Hardy."

My face feels frozen in what has to be a look of sheer disgust, given the twitch of my muscles tightening up. "That's fucked up, Harv."

"You know what I mean. And Beth is totally cool with it. She's hoping you're in."

I stop wiping the counter and lean in nice and close, with a smile plastered on my face. "Harv? If this was the zombie apocalypse, and yours was the last dick on earth, I'd cut it off and feed it to the zombies to buy me some time."

"That's cold, Nola. Real cold. You'll come around, though." Bottom lip caught between his teeth, he winks. "I'm good at wearing women down."

I shake my head and glance to the side, where Bethany's waving me over, still sitting across from Simon. Even if he's a slight bit more awkward than Harv, I'll take his company, any day, over Beth's creepy husband.

With heavy, aching feet, I hobble over to their table and lean my ass against the booth beside Bethany.

"Nola! You gotta hear this! Simon says that cryptocurrency is hot right now. Like the return on investment is insane."

Return on investment? That doesn't sound like a Bethany thing to say.

"Simon says, huh?" Holding back a snort, I catch the twitch of Simon's lips overtop of the daisy inside a vase, set in the middle of the table.

Dale insists that fresh flowers placed at every table, every day, makes his joint less of a greasy spoon.

"I don't even know what all that cryptocrap is," I add, shrugging my shoulders.

"It's the currency that drug dealers and hitmen use." Bethany's fascinated tone leaves me to wonder how much she really gives a shit about crypto, versus the tip she'll be getting for serving Simon his usual grilled cheese and fries.

"Ah, well, I forgot to renew my hitman card this year, so I guess I'm not eligible." I turn to leave, but pause at the sound of Simon clearing his throat.

He rarely makes eye contact with anyone, so when I twist back around, I'm surprised to see him looking up at me. "It's a relatively small investment. I've turned as little as fifty dollars into thousands. If you'd like, I can set you up with an account. The lingo is a little daunting at first, but the more you play with it, the better you'll become."

"That's what I've been telling her, Simon." Bethany shoots me a wink, and I roll my eyes, shaking my head at yet another sex reference. One Simon doesn't seem to pick up on. "So are we on for this weekend? You show me how to work it, and I'll play with it?"

Ugh, this conversation is nearly as bad as the one with Harv. The two of them could probably start their own cheesy dictionary of sexual puns.

Simon adjusts his glasses, his cheeks three shades of red.

Maybe he caught on, after all. "Certainly, I'm happy to get you started with an account."

"You should come over, too, Nola. We'll make it a crypto party."

With a huff, I push away from the booth and knock my knuckles on the wooden table. "As thrilling as that sounds, I'm gonna pass. Thanks, anyway, Simon."

"Sure. If you change your mind, there are plenty of tutorials that show you how to set everything up."

"Cool. Thanks."

I want to ask him why, if it's worked so well for him, is he still dressing like a prep school reject and eating grilled cheese at a greasy spoon every day. But I suppose some people are just happy where they're at in life, and he certainly seems to be content.

My shift drags on into the evening, and when it's finally time to go, I can hardly stand the walk to my car. The heels of my shoes bite into my skin as I limp across the mostly empty lot toward my car. Lara, one of the waitresses, zips by in her compact little sedan, waving at me when she passes.

An obnoxious slam from behind signals one of the busboys tossing a bag of garbage into a nearby dumpster, before heading back inside the diner.

An eerie quiet looms in the shadows across the lot as I shuffle toward my car.

Plastered to my windshield, a strip of red paper flaps against the glass, and I tilt my head, eyes narrowed, trying to make out what it might be.

The blare of a horn steels my muscles, and I turn to see Harv and Bethany roll past in their creepy white panel van I often tease looks like something a serial killer would drive. The sight of Harv blowing me a kiss through the window has my lip crimping.

Tugging the paper out of the wipers, I wait until I've

fallen into the driver's seat before opening it to the words typed across.

If given the choice, would you prefer to be strangled in your vehicle, or raped against the hood of it?

Breath whooshes out of me, and I snap my head to the rearview mirror, to find no one staring back at me, and when I peer over the backseat to be sure, I click the lock on the doors. The surrounding lot is empty. Not a single hint of movement. It's only when I stare back down at the note in my hand that I realize I'm trembling. Flipping it over to the back reveals *Sweet Dreams.*

One more glance over the backseat confirms no one is inside, and with both hands gripping the steering wheel, I attempt to settle my rattled nerves.

It's then that a recent conversation comes to mind, one Bethany told me about weeks ago, when she decided to follow me outside for a smoke. Apparently, swinging with random men and women hasn't been enough excitement for her sex life, so she and Harv decided to spice things up, by having someone rape her as he watched. Role-playing, of course, but according to her, it was the most exciting thing she's ever done. It wouldn't surprise me if the two decided to step it up a notch.

Too far, Harv. Way too far.

"Idiot," I mumble, firing up my car. It isn't enough that the asshole harasses me during my shift, but he's gotta creep me the hell out on top of it.

Sunday is my next shift with Beth, and she's going to hear about this, because I don't take this crap lightly—not anymore. I'm sure Jonah would be happy to send an officer out make Harv shit his pants a little.

5

NOLA

A thick chill settles into my chest, as I look around at surrounding graffiti-spattered walls wherein I watched Oliver disappear. Distant screams add an ominous quality to the dark and peculiar corridor ahead. Shiny white-tiled floors carry red smears and handprints of what looks like blood.

"Oliver?" My voice reverberates off the walls in a harrowing calm. Something tells me this place—a hospital, judging by the tipped over stretchers and rooms with medical-looking equipment—is the kind of place that swallows fears, glutting on every moment of dread it can reap. "Oliver, answer me!"

My heart sits heavy in my chest, as my mind tries to convince me those screams are not my son's. The heart knows better, though. It remembers breaking, when I first dropped Oliver off at Kindergarten and he reached for me, begging me to take him home. It remembers the day he fell out of a tree and broke his arm in the backyard. And the nights he's woken from nightmares, certain that monsters have come for him.

"Mom!"

It's been months since I last heard him call out for me, and *my heart sings at the sound of it, drawing my feet toward a door at the end of the long hallway. Something tells me to turn back, to stay away from that door, but I can't. Not if my son is there.*

"Go back!" The whispers are almost deafening, and with my hand on the knob, I clamp my eyes shut.

"No," I answer, opening the door.

I find my son lying in a pool of blood on the floor, his stomach sliced open, chest to navel.

"Sweet dreams," another voice whispers from behind. One I don't recognize.

"No!"

I jolt to a sitting position, my heart slamming against my ribs, as I claw through sheets, scrambling from the bed. Body shaking, I make my way down the hall toward Oliver's room and punch through the door to find his bed is empty. It's only then that I realize I forgot my knife from under my pillow, but I don't need it.

Why don't I need it?

A brief moment of confusion fades into the realization that he's not here. He's at Jonah's. Safe. I know this because I FaceTimed him earlier in the night, and I have the urge to do it again, but a glance at the clock shows two in the morning.

Resting my forehead against the doorframe, I let the agony of my nightmare settle over me. Every dream is a different scenario, aside from the split open belly. That's apparently what the drug dealers did to Denny, and from what I've gathered from the therapist and Oliver's drawings, my son watched it happen. The only prints on the weapon belonged to a known meth-head, who, of course, swore up and down he didn't do it. The dead body didn't deter him from swiping Denny's wallet, though.

Jonah once asked me if Denny'd had any connections to the cartels, as that kind of mutilation was a fairly common retribution, but I wouldn't have known. In fact, I didn't know much of anything about Denny, it seems. I didn't know he slept on the couch so he could sneak out in the middle of the night, but it made sense. According to some witnesses, and friends I had no clue Denny kept with, he was pretty active on the streets after hours. A few had even seen my son tag along with him on the nights I worked late at the diner. I suppose Oliver's silence about that was to keep the two of us from fighting.

And there I was, struggling for years to keep Band-Aids over something too broken to fix.

I can't fall back asleep, not after that dream, so I make my way down to the first floor, past the kitchen to the breezeway that leads to my mother's old pottery room.

My dad had it built for her after my older sister went missing. I was only eleven at the time, but I remember every detail of that day, leading up to the moment one of my dad's police buddies came to our door, telling us she was nowhere to be found. I can still smell the strawberry scent of her shampoo filling the air, as she brushed her hair at the vanity, while I stood by watching. I remember the infinity necklace she wore around her neck, which Dad had given us for Christmas that year. The red sweater that clung to her busty chest, making me wonder if I'd be as curvy and beautiful as she was, someday. I remember the gleam in her eyes when she talked about the boy she'd met, and the little tryst she'd organized for later that night, about which I swore I wouldn't say a word to Mom and Dad. It wasn't until that moment, when the officer had to hold my dad up to keep him from collapsing, that I finally spoke about it. When I realized it was no longer about secrets kept between sisters, but clues leading to her whereabouts.

The whole community got involved to help find Nora, but her disappearance would forever remain a mystery to my mother, who eventually became a neurotic mess.

I look around at the pottery lining the shelves—the results of hours she spent distracting her mind. On the bench below the shelves sits two halves of a vase I accidentally broke while dusting her shelves the day before.

Pulling up a stool, I squeeze a small bit of the nearby glue and epoxy into a glass dish I set out earlier, and mix it around, before adding the gold powder. With a small wooden stick, I apply the mixture along the edge of the break in a thick coating, a process known as *Kintsugi*. My Nan learned it, while traveling through Japan as a young globe-trotter, and taught it to my mother, who eventually taught it to me. Perhaps the only time spent with my mother that I truly cherished.

The philosophy behind it is a celebration of an object's history and struggles, beautifying its brokenness and cracks with delicate gold veins that tell its story. I always found it fitting for my mother, while she mourned the disappearance of my sister. Wearing her pain like the cracks in her pottery.

Over time, I became better at it, creating art from broken pieces.

Once the glue has dried, I shave away the bits sticking up from the crack and mix more of the gold filling, then apply it to the outer side of the crack. When that's dried, I'll eventually take a fine point brush and paint the crack, shave it again and apply the gold to a fine line painted over the surface. By then, I should have a much steadier hand than I do after my earlier nightmare.

It's after four, and I need to get at least another hour, or I'll spend the day looking like I suffer from narcolepsy. And, if I'm going to have a man renting out the room behind my house, I definitely need to have my wits about me tomorrow, when I meet him.

NOLA

Sunlight hits my face, and I squint against the invading brightness, slapping the back of my hand across my eyes to shield it out. With a groan, I turn over in bed, the red digital letters on my clock slowly coming into view.

9:50.

"Oh shit!" I scramble over the edge, knocking my elbow on the nightstand, and hobble to the bathroom. Even in a half-daze, my reflection is a ridiculous mess of a woman who clearly didn't get enough sleep. My hair looks like birds played in it all night, so I nab a couple bobby pins to tame it. A quick dab of concealer hides the dark circles, and I squirt toothpaste onto my toothbrush, relieving myself as I scour my teeth.

A chime from downstairs skates down my spine, as I spit foamy toothpaste into the sink. "One second!" Yelling from upstairs is futile, though. This house is like a fortress with its insulated walls, so thick I could probably die *and* decompose in here before someone ever found me.

Racing back to the bedroom, I throw on a pair of jeans

and nab the first top I see from the armoire, only realizing it's Oliver's *Star Wars* T-shirt once it's over my head and my arm is halfway through the sleeve.

"Fuck!" I cross my arms to yank it off, but I can't get my elbow back through the hole, leaving my arm dangling above my head. "Fuck! Fuck! Fuck!"

Another ring of the bell is really just obnoxious at this point, and my mood flips from panicked to frustrated, as I wrangle my other arm into its sleeve. The tearing sound mirrors my slowly unraveling calm, and I tug the shirt as far over my exposed navel as I can, then pause, wondering if I should grab my knife. "What are you gonna do, stab the guy you invited over?" I mutter, jogging down the staircase.

One more ring of the bell grates at my nerves, and I throw back the door. "I'm coming, goddammit!"

Standing on my front porch is a man over six feet tall, in a sleek black suit. Two of me could span the width of him, and above his crisp black collar sits a snake tattoo that winds up his neck. With dark hair, and cold, gray eyes that sweep down over my outfit, he's both handsome and intimidating, but the scar across his face adds an edge of menace, sending up red flags.

He doesn't look like a potential tenant. He looks like danger, wrapped in a nice suit.

Not happening. I've already decided this deal is off.

"I'm here about the apartment. We spoke yesterday." His eyes trail down again and back, and I suddenly remember I'm wearing an eleven-year-old's favorite T-shirt.

"Yeah. I'm ... Nola." Yes, I was named after the city where my mom and dad apparently got it on in their forties, resulting in an *oops* baby. My miraculous conception to a mother who was shitfaced and horny. Reaching out a hand, I give one more yank at the hem of the T-shirt and flinch at another tear. "Forgive me, I was ..." I don't even have huge boobs, but they look monstrous in this T-shirt, pressing against the fabric like they're trying to make a break for it.

"Firm," he says in a velvet voice, returning the handshake.

"Excuse me?"

"Your grip." Twisting our clutched hands, he seems to examine them clasped together, his big palm swallowing mine. "Strong."

Clearing my throat, I slip my hand from his and give the too-small T-shirt one more tug. I can't have this guy roaming around my property. The neighbors are going to think I've taken up with the mafia.

"Look, you're a few minutes late. I actually rented out the apartment about an hour ago to a … *person* who made an appointment before you did."

"I'll pay double what the other *person* paid. I'm guessing a woman."

This guy is relentless. And even if his offer has leaped into the realm of ridiculous, he's starting to piss me off.

"Why do you presume I'm sexist?" I rest my hands on my hips, frowning back up at him.

"I can only imagine what you're presuming right now." His eyes take another dip south and linger on the return trip. "Can I at least see what I'm missing out on?"

"What's the point? It belongs to someone else."

"Does it?"

I can't tell if he's talking about the apartment, or me. He should shack up with Harv and Bethany and start a university of sexual puns.

"Fine. I'll let you check it out." Hell, maybe when he sees it, he'll lose interest. Surely, this guy wouldn't be happy living in a tiny in-law suite that barely has cable. "I've got nothing else to accomplish today." I usher him inside, taking in the size of him as he passes me in the doorway. This dude could crumple me into a ball and toss me out the window, if he was feeling ambitious enough.

"Straight out the back," I say, guiding him down the corridor to the mudroom. The kitchen passes us on the left where the breezeway stands open, and I catch his quick glance toward it.

"You don't strike me as a *Star Wars* fan," he says over his shoulder, as he comes to a stop in front of the door leading out to the back yard.

"Who's passing judgment now?" I wait for him to open the door and step out onto the deck.

The back of the property is probably the most appealing part of the house. My father wanted to create a sanctuary for my mother, so he planted trees that provided enough privacy from the neighbors and shaded the many gardens I've done a piss-poor job of keeping maintained in recent years.

"For your information, it's my son's shirt. If you hadn't been doorbell happy this morning, I might've had time to grab a shirt that fits." Realizing I offered information I didn't care to divulge, about my son, I bite my cheek and inwardly kick myself.

"Do you always wear your son's clothes?"

"No. But if I did, that's none of your business."

The in-law suite sits above the three-car, detached garage behind the house, with a narrow deck that spans the width of it, and a staircase at the far right of the structure. At the foot of the stairs, I take the lead, certain the guy is staring at my ass as we ascend toward the door of the apartment.

"I have to say, the view in the back is incredible."

Swinging around, I frown down at him, nearly losing my balance when I see he's waited at the bottom of the staircase and is staring out over the yard. "Oh. Yeah, my father was better at keeping it maintained."

"Your mom didn't keep up the yard?"

"No. That was my father's job."

"How sexist."

Huffing my frustration, I damn near slam through the door to the in-law apartment, and I stand in the center of it, arms crossed, waiting for him to enter. Once inside, his eyes scan over everything. And I do mean everything, as he opens the cupboards, the closets, and ventures into the bedroom.

"Nice. I'm sorry I didn't claim it first."

"Well, better luck next time."

"You did disclose that you have a massive water leak, right?"

"What?"

He points above me, toward where an enormous brown spot discolors the once stark-white ceiling. "That's going to be a problem later. Expensive one. You also have seal failure going on in the windows. That's why there's condensation inside the panes. The insulation out here feels a little thin, as well. No renter is going to want to deal with a potential disaster. I'm guessing *he, or she* is aware and doesn't have an issue with all these things, though."

Shit. I haven't spent any significant time out here, aside from a quick cleaning I did before posting the ad for a renter, and I guess I failed to notice the maintenance it needed. Doesn't help that my husband didn't do shit for home repairs, when he was alive.

"Thanks. I'd have taken it, in spite of all that, but I suppose that ship has passed. Nice meeting you, *Star Wars*."

Star Wars. Indignation needles me in the gut, as I watch him exit the apartment, my mind rapidly contemplating my options. If I don't rent it out, Oliver's going to get whatever is left after bills every month for Christmas presents, which is little more than zero. I could use the two hundred Jonah and Diane gave me, but that'll leave us eating ramen noodles, when the gas bill comes due at the end of the month.

Which means I could rent it out to someone who'll probably swindle me down, once they see all the shit that needs repair.

Or I could let Mafia Man pay me four times the rent and skate comfortably into the New Year.

Goddamn it, Nola.

"Wait."

He's already halfway down the stairs, when I hustle toward the door to catch him.

"Wait." With a contemplative huff, I scratch the back of my head. "What's the suit all about? What do you do?"

"I work in securities."

"Like a mall cop?"

"Like stocks and bonds."

"Oh! Right. Those kind of securities." Not that I'd know the first thing about that. "And the tattoos are … *not* gang related?"

"No."

Whatever piss poor interview I'm conducting right now, he's at least humoring me with decent answers.

"What does a businessman like yourself want with some old, rundown, in-law apartment with a leaky roof? It doesn't make sense. Shouldn't you be living it up at the Ritz-Carlton downtown?"

"I'm a man who values his privacy, above all else. My stay in the Chicago area is temporary. I'm hoping to concentrate on work without the distraction of the city."

"And you're not some creep who keeps bottles of Jergens to *put the lotion on it's skin.*"

"Do you have something against Jergens?"

"What I have is a son. And I've really struggled to hold my faith in humanity over the last few years. Please don't make me regret changing my mind and letting you take the apartment. You're still willing to pay double?"

"Triple, if I can occupy the space in the next hour."

Jesus Christ. Triple would let me take Christmas week off work—something I haven't done since Oliver was a baby.

"I can't. At this point, I'd just be taking advantage of you."

"I guilt-tripped you into renting your apartment to me, so I guess that makes us even."

I scratch the back of my head again, trying not to let the lure of money talk me into something stupid, but the lure of money is definitely talking me into something stupid. "Right. So … um. I didn't catch your name."

"Everyone calls me Voss."

"Well, what does the DMV call you, because I need to run a quick background check before we do this."

"Rhett Voss."

Rhett Voss sounds like something out of a romance novel. "Are you from here originally, *Voss*?"

"New York. *Star Wars*."

My eye twitches at that, and I roll my shoulders, tugging the hem one more time. Of course he's from New York. Fancy city to match his fancy suit and his fancy car. And here I'm standing in jeans, with no shoes, and an eleven year-old's *Star Wars* shirt. "Can you come back in about a half hour?"

"Sure. Only if you promise to answer the door."

"Of course."

Instead, the guy waits in his car—a fancy black Audi parked at the curb, which I'll have to inform him is jack-bait in this neighborhood. Not that this part of the city is all that bad, but his car doesn't scream drug dealer, it screams stock trader, so it's basically fair game around here.

I call Jonah, who has one of his buddies run the guy's name and plates.

Turns out, he actually is from New York. Actually, a stock trader. And, more surprising than all of that, *doesn't* have a criminal history whatsoever. In fact, his record is as polished as the goddamn paint job on that car.

"Are you sure, Jonah?" I ask, staring down at all my notes. "Not even a speeding ticket, parking ticket, nothing?"

"Squeaky clean, according to Tanner."

Which means I have no reason not to trust this guy. Damn it. The lure is growing stronger by the minute.

"How's Oliver?"

"Great! He and Diane went out for some takeout sushi for his last night here."

"Awesome. He used to love sushi." Sometimes, I wonder what Oli would turn out like if I just let him live with my brother and his wife, instead of his spending so much time by himself. I wonder if living with me is going to fuck him up for the rest of his life. Turn him into one of those kids who guns down his classmates, because no one knew how lonely he was. "Thanks for taking him, Jonah. You guys are the best."

"Ah, this is all Diane's doing. She's been planning this weekend for weeks now."

Well, that's a relief. It's somewhat comforting to know the things that were once just everyday life for Jonah and me take weeks to plan for someone else. "Okay, I guess I need to tell this guy he's good to move in."

"Don't feel like you have to do this … letting some stranger into the home. You have choices, Nola. Diane and I are—"

"Nope. I'm not going to keep relying on someone else for everything. I want to do this. I need things to loosen up around here, and … maybe it'll be good to have a guy around Oliver again."

"You don't have to recruit some *Wall Street Wolf* to do that. I'm happy to take him up to dad's cabin sometime."

"You're busy, Jonah. And soon you're going to have your own child."

"Maybe so. But that doesn't mean I won't be here for you and Oliver."

"I know. I'm going to let you go, okay? This guy's been sitting in his car, waiting for an answer. I don't want to be the one who mars his *squeaky* clean record with his first kill."

After clicking the phone off, I head out to the curb, and his window rolls down as I approach. Big surprise, the car interior is black leather, and the technology looks like something straight out of a cockpit. The scent from inside wafts passed me: leather and cologne, and that new car smell beneath it all.

"Looks like you're set to move in. Your background checks out."

"Fantastic."

"So ... I guess I'll let you get to it. Can I get you something to drink?" I glance down at the fancy Fiji bottle sitting in his drink holder.

"No, thank you." Climbing out of the vehicle, he takes a moment to adjust his suit, and pops the trunk of his car. Tucked inside are two large, shiny black Tumi cases that he removes with ease.

"Looks like you don't have much to carry, so I'll let you get settled on your own."

"Perfect."

"Right."

"Do I get a set of keys?"

"Oh!" I stuff my hand into my pocket, where I put them before calling Jonah, and hand him a set. "There's room in the garage for your car. I don't use it, but ... my car is nowhere near as fancy as yours. Um ... no parties, no ... drug deals, or prostitutes in and out of here."

Face screwed up into an amused sort of smirk, he slams the trunk shut.

"I'm serious. I got enough shit going on. I don't need my son asking *those* questions."

"You've nothing to worry about. As I said, I keep to myself."

"Good. Because as much as you value your privacy, I value my peace and quiet."

"Good. Sounds like we're a match made in heaven. I'll let you get to your peace and quiet, while I settle into my privacy now."

Perhaps it's his matter-of-fact attitude that has me feeling frustrated in all of this. From the moment I talked to the guy, his voice resonated the kind of arrogance and confidence I loathe in men. Probably wouldn't bother me near as much, if he weren't good looking on top of it, in a rugged, career criminal sort of way.

I trail my gaze after him as he strolls off toward the back-yard, carrying his suitcases that probably cost more than my entire wardrobe is worth. A glance down at the *Star Wars* shirt shows a chocolate stain just above the nipple, and I groan.

7

VOSS

Nola Tensley is a twenty-eight-year-old single mother, whose husband was murdered in what was deemed to be a drug-related incident. Though, aside from some meth-head they picked up nearby, they really didn't nail down too many suspects. Nola Tensley graduated top of her class and was accepted to a number of universities, all of which she rejected—likely due to pregnancy at a young age, I guess. She's a long time waitress at Duli's Diner, and dabbles in ceramics as a side gig.

Nola Tensley is also fucking delectable—a potential distraction I didn't anticipate when I first stumbled upon her ad for a renter. With brown hair and those chestnut colored eyes Carl apparently wants to add to his hobby room of horrors, she's not at all what I expected. A little spitfire who stirred my blood the moment I saw her in that too-tight T-shirt.

I toss her file onto the worn-down coffee table in front of me. The paisley patterned couch beneath me is surprisingly intact, and doesn't smell particularly old and moldy, like the rest of the place. The outdated décor may lack the luxuries and technology I've grown accustomed to, but I wouldn't have passed it up for anything. It's here that I'll track down and find what I'm looking for.

And so long as Nola Tensley minds her own business, I'll not pose any threat to her, or her son. I've killed for lesser infractions than going through my things, and I won't hesitate to guard that identity with my life.

After all, I've spent a lifetime in both the military and working for The Gallows, keeping below the radar, concealing my true identity. As far as the world is concerned, Rhett Voss is a highly successful stock trader in New York, visiting Chicago on temporary business.

I asked Jackson to find as much information on the woman as he could possibly gather—a request he was happy to oblige in, in order to keep me from hunting him down after fucking up my last job. Turns out, though, there isn't a whole lot on the woman, and her file came back surprisingly thin. Of course, Jackson hasn't always been the most thorough at gathering information, which will leave me to do some of the work on my own. Mostly, I like to know what I'm dealing with when it comes to the people I encounter, even if its not all business.

Unlike half the women her age, who've already bled the majority of their lives into social media, Nola hasn't logged into her Facebook account in a year, nor is she listed in the White Pages online. No speeding tickets, or overdue library fines to speak of. Not even those annoying public records sites that claim to possess all I want to know about Nola Tensley have her shit right.

She's kept herself off the radar, too.

Progress notes from Insight Outpatient Psychiatry, the only source of information available on her, lay strewn over the table, detailing Nola's six consecutive sessions with her psychiatrist. Nothing more than breadcrumbs of information she was willing to divulge, during her appointments, that don't add up to much of a picture about the woman. I'm left knowing very little about her, including why she stopped seeing her psychiatrist a few months back, and why she wakes up from nightmares every night. Doesn't make much sense that she'd step outside of her airtight little box to allow a total stranger into her carefully guarded world, but I'm guessing her need for cash outweighs her desire to remain unnoticed.

Most times, Jackson's findings are sufficient enough for me to piece together the missing parts, but all his research has done is leave me with more curiosity about the woman. Unfortunately, she's not the only reason I'm here.

The chime of my cellphone draws my attention to a message notification on the screen. I open it to the same encrypted address as before.

If you wish to play, follow the link to your first clue. Doing so will trigger release of the funds into your account.

He can't be foolish enough to think clicking on the link will provide access to my IP address, unless he believes I'm a total idiot. I click on the link as instructed, which opens to a blank page. An image begins to load, slow and tediously, as if the file is too large. It's a picture of my mother, who must've been eighteen at the time, given the youth of her eyes. A cloth is draped over her shoulder, where she sits on a crushed red velvet couch that I remember from childhood, and my tiny feet are sticking out of the right side of the cloth as she breastfeeds me. It's a photo I recognize from the thick album of baby pictures she kept in the closet. As the picture loads from the top down, more details come through in remarkable clarity. The wallpaper behind her, covered in cowboys and stagecoaches, that I used to stare at during long hours of punishment.

Frowning, I stare back at the screen, trying to tease the ways a baby picture might be a clue.

And? I type back to him.

Eyes collect the truth that the mind chooses not to see.

I click on the photograph again, realizing there's something in it I'm just not picking up. Everything is as I remember in the photograph. The walls. The coffee table that always held magazines and the TV Guide. The couch. My mother. Me. That's it. Zooming in on each detail fails to reveal anything out of the ordinary.

I refuse to let him believe he's stumped me on the first clue, so, for now, I click out of the image and resign myself to come back to it again later.

Tell me what happens in three weeks.

I win the game.

How?

You see? You remember how to play this one. You die a relatively benign death. Afterward, I watch you sink to the bottom of the river.

There was a time threats like that would scare the absolute shit out of me. Back when he was so much bigger than me and my world was so much smaller. I've seen too much death since, to be rattled by his words. Gruesome demises that make me wonder just how different the two of us really are.

Funny, I say in response. *It was you I watched sink the last time we played.*

His lack of reply tells me I've pissed him off. Last thing an egotistical psychopath like him wants to hear about is how the weak and gangly kid he inherited grew up to be a worthy opponent. The thought puts a smile on my face as I swipe out of my messages, giving one last mental tease of the image he sent to me.

Carl works in puzzles starting from the middle. He

doesn't frame the image in a way that's helpful, or obvious, and I can only imagine the answer will hit me at some random moment, so no point dwelling on one piece when I have an entire jigsaw to figure out in the next few weeks.

It's a shame police aren't smart enough to track him down, but I suppose that's what makes him such a formidable rival, what sends a jolt of excitement through my veins. He doesn't make himself an easy kill.

I gather the file into a pile and dump Nola's medical records into my briefcase, then lock it up and slide it beneath the coffee table.

Inside the fridge are three days of meals that I ordered from a chef in New York who prepares clean, organic foods. It's enough until I find a suitable replacement here, or do the cooking myself. I eat a goat cheese and prosciutto sandwich with the basil pesto included in a small side cup, before I head out to the one place I've avoided since the night I escaped seventeen years ago.

The house where I grew up.

The dilapidated fascia board dangles from the massive roof, slamming against the worn-down, chipped brick of the home, whose interior walls kept me imprisoned most of my teenage years. The Jansen estate was something of a landmark, years before my grandfather took over, having inherited it from his father, who made a fortune in the meat-packing business. The once-stately tudor mansion might've belonged to me after my grandfather died, if he hadn't been such a selfish, greedy prick. Instead, millions of dollars went to the state, and the property went to shit, it seems.

The surrounding neighborhood is quiet and dark, not as active these days, judging by the unkempt yards and rotted exteriors that haven't been properly maintained for the kind of money these houses boast.

Beyond the busted iron gate, I flick my cigarette away and make my way up the cracked driveway, over the weeds sticking up from the slivers in the concrete. High gables slice up toward the night sky, through the looming canopy of a nearby beech tree, like two silent opponents fallen into an eternal rest.

Place is still creepy as shit after all these years.

The kids had a rhyme they used to sing about it after my mom died here. Something about the *monsters inside pulling you in, never to be seen again.*

I'm pretty sure they had no clue my mom died, as my grandfather only reported her as *missing* to police, and so began the rumor that she was placed in a mental institution, to coincide with their cute little songs about the house.

The times I went to school, I got teased relentlessly about how she lost it after I was born. "*One look at your ugly face, and she went bonkers,*" they said. If only it had been that simple. I'd have preferred that end, in lieu of her suffering.

If only they knew the truth was far worse than what they imagined.

Lies are so much easier, though. Not as cold and bitter. Terrifying. Lies don't slither down your throat, into your belly, eating you from the inside out, the way the truth does. Instead, they remain at the tip of the tongue, loaded and ready to spew at the first police officer who asks what really happened that night.

I didn't tell them what I witnessed, for fear my grandfather would see to it that I became the next victim buried in the woods behind the property.

The screen door, half-cocked on its hinges, creaks when I open it with steady hands. Sometimes, I wish my pulse would race, that my body would tremble at the thought of facing so many horrific memories. At least then I'd feel human. When a man has lived his entire life as a monster, though, nothing really scares him anymore. Not even the darkest demons from his past.

The open, empty parlor beyond the front door stirs my blood like ghosts rousing from dormancy to greet me. I can damn near taste the copper on my tongue, as I move deeper into the house, the stench of death still clinging to the air. Moonlight casts lines on the wooden floors, cutting through the metal bars across the windows. Security bars, thought to keep intruders from getting in, but I knew better, even back then. They were placed there to keep anyone inside from getting out.

The kitchen stands equally empty, its cupboards open with broken panels, which suggest it's been raided at one time. I'm not sure what happened to the sparse furniture that once decorated the shithole, but it's gone, including my mother's upright piano—the only thing I regret leaving behind.

I'm surprised the place still stands after all these years. I'd have thought the neighbors would've burned it down, with all the negative gossip surrounding it.

Down the hall stands a closet, one I remember more intimately than I care to. A faded brass knob squeals with a slow turn, and I peel back the first layer of my fucked up childhood.

Pressure beats inside my skull, into my sinuses, like a water balloon about to pop. Everything is black, and the thin twine of rope bites into my wrists, dangling over my head. On the other side of the door, Carl keeps count. Six hundred twenty-three, six hundred twenty-four, six hundred twenty-five ... *My punishment for tattling about the dead cat in the shed is three thousand seconds upside down in the closet, blindfolded with my hands tied.*

I hate when my mother leaves me home alone with him. I dread the nights she ventures into the city with grandfather until late, and I become Carl's little guinea pig.

Six hundred thirty-nine, six hundred forty … *he keeps on, ticking off the seconds of my life that don't matter to him. Everyone says there's something wrong with him, but Mother doesn't care. He's her baby brother, but only a few years older than me, which means I know more than my mom about what he does when no one else is around. How he skinned that cat alive and burned it with grandpa's blowtorch. I can still hear it screaming inside my head, even now, over the irritating sound of Carl's counting.*

I only hope grandfather doesn't come home soon, because if he finds me this way, he'll beat Carl, which will only mean more torture for me the next time mother leaves. Carl's afraid of grandfather. I am, too, the way he smacks my mom around. Makes me wish I was bigger, so I could punch him right into the wall. I'd punch Carl, too, since he tells me someday he's going to kill all of us and burn the house down.

Not if I kill him first.

On the top shelf sits the old, dust-coated album, filled with the only baby pictures my mother ever took of me. Some nights, they were my bedtime stories, and she'd sit flipping through them, telling me stories behind each one. Her favorite was the Navy picture of my dad, who apparently died during one of his tours overseas. She told me of the letters she wrote to him, and continued to write even after he died, detailing my childhood milestones. She kept them tucked away in a shoebox, until my grandfather found them and tossed them into a burn barrel out back. I remember her sobbing over the small bits of ash and embers, cursing her own father for destroying her life.

Halfway through the book, I pause at the place where the image of my mother sitting on the crushed velvet couch should be. In its place is a pack of matches for a motel up on Kedzie that I slide out of the yellowing plastic sheath. Flipping it open reveals a number—room number, at a guess—and I tuck the matches into my back pocket.

Clue Number 1.

I should leave at this point, but the door at the end of the hallway taunts me to open it.

Don't leave me here, a soft voice chimes in my ear, and I feel the first chill wind down my spine.

Album tucked beneath my arm, I stride toward it, the view flipping before my eyes, from the ruined and peeling paint, to the smooth dark brown that almost looked like a void there when I was a kid.

I can hear Carl's record player, *Master of Puppets* by Metallica, one of his favorites that he only played when grandfather wasn't around.

I keep my eyes on the door, praying he doesn't catch me before I reach it. Turning the knob opens the void to the staircase that leads to the cellar of the house. I click my flashlight on, letting the arc of light slice through the darkness below, and close the door behind me as I begin my descent. Only Carl ever ventures down here, guarding the cellar as if he's got the secrets to the universe locked away. Grandfather doesn't bother with the stairs since his knees have gone out on him. Not like anyone in this house would call for help, if he happened to fall down the staircase.

The air is colder, musty and thick with the scent of rot. My breaths arrive faster, sucking it into my lungs, as I fear what lies on the other side of the concrete wall ahead of me. With careful steps, I approach, but pause at a clinking sound, before rounding the wall brings me to a dark open pantry, where grandpa used to store his paint and tools.

Mostly empty shelves line the walls, and I scan the flashlight down to a silver bowl on the floor to the left of me, filled with water. Like a dog's bowl. The concrete around it's wet. My heart pounds inside my chest, more so when I lift my flashlight to the face of a girl, maybe eighteen or nineteen, judging by her size. She's propped against the wall, wearing what looks like my dead mother's favorite dress. Over her eyes is a black blindfold, and I watch as her lip quivers, as though she might cry.

"Who are you?" I whisper in the darkness.

"Please. I want to go home. Please, let me go home."

Whoever she is, she doesn't deserve to be kept down here like some kind of animal "Sure. Just ... follow me."

"I can't."

"I'll remove your blindfold."

"It's not just my blindfold."

It's then I notice her arms resting at her side and her legs twisted oddly beneath her. "Are they broken?"

"I don't think so. I can't move them, though." Her lip quivers beneath the blindfold. "I think ... I think he gave me some kind of ... drug, or something."

I edge closer until crouching in front of her, and her trembling heightens. A small streak of red peeks out from the blindfold, and when I attempt to lift it from her eyes, she flinches, turning her head away.

"It's okay. I'm just going to remove it."

Head still wobbly, she turns back toward me, and I lift it up over her cheekbones to reveal a slice across her eye that's red and bloodshot, making her pupils wide and evil-looking.

Dropping the flashlight to the floor, I kick back away from her, watching her fall onto her shoulder.

"Please! Don't leave me! Don't leave me!"

Eyes squinting, I peer around the empty room where I found the girl. All that remains are scattered water stains on the wall, and that lingering scent of mold. My flashlight scans over the windows, still blackened by the cloth Carl used to block out the view, tattered and hardly clinging to the glass anymore.

I didn't even know the girls name, or how she ended up in the cellar. All I knew at the time was how sadistic my uncle had become, and how his therapists had grossly under-estimated his level of fucked-upness.

A thump overhead steels my muscles, and I set my hand on the gun at my hip, listening to what sounds like move-ment on the first floor. I make my way back up the staircase, stepping light to avoid any sounds. Flicking off the flashlight, I tuck it into my pocket and stalk down the hallway, letting my Glock lead the way.

Adrenaline moves through me in waves at the thought of coming face to face with Carl again. I've damn near fanta-sized about this moment.

Stopping at the closet door, I peek around the corner to the kitchen, which sits approximately above where I stood in the cellar.

Empty.

Something brushes against my leg, and I aim my gun to the floor, but steady myself when a black mass scampers behind me. I reach down and lift a small, black kitten from between my feet.

"Where'd you come from?" I mutter over its soft meow-ing. Thing looks like it hasn't eaten in a few days with its bones poking through patchy black fur. No tag, or collar, or anything. I set it back down on the floor and shove my gun back into its holster, with the photo album still tucked beneath my arm.

A pinprick needles my shin as the cat claws up my trousers.

"Hey, hey." I detach him from my pants to keep him from snagging the fabric, and the little bastard just meows back at me, as I dangle him in front of my face. "I don't have any food for you. You're gonna have to wait for the next sucker who walks through the door."

I pause at my words. The next sucker could be a psychotic prick, and if that's the case, hunger will be the least of this cat's worries. Last time I picked up a stray and brought it home, the thing was sacrificed and skewered, with its eyeballs bobbing in a jar as a memento.

"All right, here's the deal. I feed you. I bathe you. And tomorrow morning, I'm letting you go. Got it?"

The cat meows again, still dangling by its scruff.

"Fucking bleeding hearts." I exit the house, suddenly remembering the Audi's upholstery, and stare down at the cat. "You put one hole in my leather seats, cat, and I'll put one hole in your head."

8

NOLA

D ecked out in jammies, I'm flipping through TV Channels when headlights crawl up the driveway. On instinct, I peek out the window, catching the tail end of the Audi, as it makes it way toward the garage. It's while settling back onto the couch that I notice the slight trembling of my muscles.

Gotta get used to this.

As usual, all the doors to the house are locked, and Oliver won't be back until tomorrow morning, which is good, in case the guy decides to kill me in my sleep. At least my son won't have to witness both parents' deaths.

Ugh. The thought of that. Why did I do this? Why did I let a stranger into my home? Not technically *in my home*, but near enough to make me want to clutch that knife under my pillow tonight. What the hell was I thinking?

Money. Three thousand measly dollars that won't mean a damn thing, if the guy decides to gut me open for fun. Speaking of which.

I sink into the couch, slapping a hand against my forehead, and groan. "I never collected rent!" Which officially makes me the worst landlord in the history of landlords. *Shit.* What if the guy's a freeloader? Maybe that's why he drives a fancy car. He can afford it by not paying rent!

Stupid. The guy didn't do anything wrong. It was my fault for not asking for the money off the bat, but asking for anything is a problem for me, even if I'm legally permitted and expected to do so.

My phone rings with a number I don't recognize, but I answer anyway. Music pounds through the phone, over the hum of chatter, like a party at the other end.

"Nola! Can you hear me?"

Hairs on the back of my neck stand at the sound of my name through a voice I can't quite make out.

"It's Bethany! Hang on! I'll try to find somewhere a bit quieter!"

The music fades to her heavy breaths, probably as she hustles somewhere away from the noise.

"Okay, can you hear me now?"

"Yeah. How did you get my number?"

"I'm at the bar, and Dale's here! He's trashed. Buying everyone drinks!"

"Okay …. Again, how did you get my number, though?"

"Dale, duh! Get your ass up here before he sobers up and realizes his tab!" Her laughter through the phone is annoying as hell, and I wait until she stops. "I've never seen him so blitzed!"

"Hey, I have a bone to pick with you." Perhaps now isn't the time, but neither is my next shift, when I have to work with her and possibly run into Harv again. "Tell Harv the next time he threatens me, I'll have the Chicago PD pay him a little visit."

"What are you talking about?"

"The note he left on my car?"

"No idea what you're talking about. Hang on, he's right here. I'll ask him."

"No, wait—"

"Hello, Nolick. What's going on?"

"It's Nola. You know it's Nola. Quit with the shit. And while you're at it, quit leaving notes on my car. It's fucking creepy."

"I don't recall leaving a note on your car, but I'll take that into consideration."

"You don't recall asking me … a question?"

"Are you considering my offer?"

Ugh. The guy has no shame. No shame, at all. "No, you sick fuck! And if you ever threaten to strangle me, or rape me, again, your ass will be in serious jeopardy, hanging out with the gang members at the jail."

"Look, Nola. I'm a dick. And a perv. A whole lot of other things. But I never ever hurt a woman who wasn't begging me for it. That sadist shit isn't really my bag."

I don't believe that for one second, but at least now he knows I'm onto him. "Don't fuck with me, Harv."

"But I—"

I click out of the call before giving him a chance to respond.

Shit. I'm going to have to rescue Dale before he has to remortgage his home to pay for a bunch of drinks. "God-damnit!" It sucks being the only responsible adult, some-times. And since I'm already riled up, it might be a good time to ask for rent, particularly as I have to make the mort-gage payment no later than next week.

I change quickly, throwing on a sweater and jeans, then head out the back door. The lights are still on in the apart-ment as I climb the staircase and knock on the door. My palms are sweating right now, and my heart feels like its pounding against my stomach, stirring up nausea. Ever since

I was a kid, I've had issues asking for cash. I once donated plasma just to avoid asking my dad for gas money. Not that he wouldn't have given it to me, but the thought of asking just felt degrading, for some reason. This is why Denny lived essentially rent free for months before I worked up the balls to hound him about the bills, and that was only because I was seriously sinking beneath the surface in those days before his death.

The door swings open to reveal the most muscular chest I've ever seen in my life, chiseled with lean, cut muscle and a few scattered tattoos. Like looking at a real-life sculpture standing before me.

And tucked in the crook of one massive bicep is a tiny black kitten.

Mouth gaping, I tip my head and point to the small creature. "Um. Cats. Cats aren't allowed up here. Pretty sure I said no pets." I can't even look at his face after ogling his body.

"You said no *prostitutes*."

"Pets, or prostitutes."

"You never said pets."

I finally lift my gaze to his, only to offer a scowl at his annoying banter. "Well, I meant to."

The slight bit of amusement in his eyes is frustrating, given the circumstances.

"Well, you don't have to worry. I'm just feeding him, and I'll be sending him on his way first thing in the morning."

"You … you can't just feed a cat and let it go. They come back! And they tell other cats that you're a supplier, and then we have a yard full of cats that won't leave. They're like … a really shitty cold you can't kick."

"Are you suggesting I starve the cat?"

"No. I'm not. I'm just saying …"

"I should kick it?"

"Yes. I mean, no! You should call the humane society."

"To have him properly euthanized?"

With a huff, I cross my arms and glance away to keep my anger from exploding to the surface. "They'd try to adopt him first. I'm sure he'll end up in a good home."

"And if he doesn't, you're okay with his death on your shoulders?"

"Why are you giving me a hard time?"

He tips his head just enough for me to catch a glimpse of the snake tattooed across his neck. "I'm sorry. Did you need something, *Star Wars*?"

Star Wars. I'm never going to live the T-shirt thing down with this guy.

"Yes. I do." And yet, suddenly I can't bring myself to mouth the words. I can't even think to ask him for money right now, and I can feel my cheeks getting hotter by the second, at the prospect of asking.

The worst. The. Worst. Landlord in history. "To let you know I'm leaving … and … well, that's it."

"You plan to tell me every time you leave the house?"

"No. I just …. I'd feel a lot better about you staying here, if you could maybe give me a reference, or something. Just someone who can attest that you don't kill people for a living."

"My background check didn't put you at ease?"

"A little, but … my son comes back tomorrow morning, and I just want to make sure I'm not doing something stupid."

"Jackson."

"What?"

"My colleague's name is Jackson Faust."

As he reels off a number, I tug my cellphone and open the notes app, jotting it down before I forget it. "Okay. I'll wait until morning to call."

"What if I kill you before then?"

I frown. "Not funny."

"My apologies. And I'll also apologize in advance for subjecting you to Jackson."

"I'm sure he's not that bad."

"I'm sure you'll change your mind after speaking with him. Now, if you don't mind, I have to bathe this cat before I kick him."

"I didn't say … kick him. He's cute." I reach out to pet the kitten, whose little paws wrap around my fingers, pulling it to his teeth. "Ouch!"

"Probably still a little hungry." Voss snatches my hand, as I draw it back, and examines my fingertip. His palms are warm and calloused and strong enough to crush my fingers. "Might want to wash that. I don't know where this cat's been."

"I bet you say that to all the girls." Sneering, I push past him into the apartment and make my way to the kitchen, taking in the scent of cologne that's officially overpowered the mold inside.

"A smartass, too, huh?"

Pumping soap onto my finger, I scrub the small scratch clean of blood and dry it with a piece of paper towel I stocked before he moved in. "Only to those I don't know anything about."

"Well, what would you like to know, Nola?"

"Do you have kids?"

"No." He scratches behind the cat's ears, letting it chew on his big fingers that probably don't feel any pain. "And no wife, in case you were curious."

"I wasn't. But while we're on the topic of curiosity, what are the tattoos about?"

With a sigh, he twists his arm and shows off the skulls inked on his bicep, once again drawing my eyes to his muscles. "Four years in the Army. Too much alcohol. Stupid decisions, mostly."

"And you don't drink excessively?"

"Define excessive."

"Passed out on a park bench, with no recollection of how you got there."

"I prefer to sleep in a bed. So, no, I guess not."

"Okay, well. That's a start." I toss the used paper towel into the nearby trashcan and cross my arms.

"What about you?" he asks, and the way he cradles the cat like a baby, playing with it, makes for an adorable distraction.

"I prefer to sleep in a bed, too."

"I meant, what is your tattoo all about?"

"When did you—" I scratch the back of my head, remembering he must've seen it on my back when I showed him the apartment. Too many painful memories associated with the rose tattooed there, though. "Maybe some other time."

"Fair enough."

"So, I'll let you get back to your kitty bath. Have a good night."

His eyes lift to mine, and for a split second, he looks like something out of a magazine. Dark, alluring, far too sexy to be living in the same place my Nan lived out her final days. "Goodnight Nola."

I arrive at the bar, really not wanting to venture inside, but I don't have much of a choice, unless I'm cool with watching Dale blow up his tab. It's crowded on a Saturday night, and loud, and smells like pennies. Everything I didn't want my Saturday night to be, but it boils my blood, the way some people can be so predatory toward decent people. Dale has always been good to his wait-staff, always looking out for us whenever a customer gets belligerent, or we've got personal shit going on. I'd have never gotten through Denny's death without Dale's patience, so it pisses me off that someone like Beth would take advantage of him that way.

My being here is solely based on principle—and the fact that Beth and Harv are already on my shit-list, for the note.

I plow through the crowd toward the two twisted love-birds, who sit laughing with Dale, Simon, and another wait-ress from the diner, Shayna.

Simon is the oddball of the group, but I'm less concerned with him, the moment I catch sight of Dale. Steps slowing as I approach, I take in my boss's condition: eyes alert, not wobbling like he's trashed, or looking the least bit troubled that he supposedly just offered drinks on the house.

"What's going on?"

All eyes turn to me, and the moment Dale shakes his head, I know I've been duped.

"She showed up! Ha! Ten bucks, Shay!" Bethany does some stupid little dance that leaves me frowning, as I try to piece the scene together. "Pay up, bitch."

At this point, my fingers are already balled into tight fists, ready to throw a punch. "You said Dale was trashed off his ass."

Dale's expression is half remorseful and half amused, and wholly irritating the shit out of me. "Sorry, Nola. Beth said it was the only way to get you to come out tonight. But *your* drinks are on me. For your trouble."

"I'll pass. Assholes." The anger is more intense than I'm letting on, but rather than go postal over it, I spin around to leave, but feel a tight grip on my arm. A quick glance back shows Bethany actually looking a slight bit rueful, though it's hard to tell under the layers of black eyeliner around her lids.

"Wait, Nola. You never hang with us anymore. Just have one drink, yeah?"

Shaking my head, I grit my teeth to keep from biting her and attempt to pry my arm loose, but she tightens her hold. "I have things to do tonight," I grit out.

"What? Watch TV until you fall asleep on the couch? When was the last time you had fun? Like, *real* fun?"

The words of my former psychologist come rushing to mind, and I drop my gaze so she doesn't get the impression I'm actually pondering her question.

"You need this, Nola. I didn't call you out because I wanted to piss you off. I knew you wouldn't come. But I also know, deep down, you miss the laughs. Remember those deep belly laughs, when we'd work late shift and swear we were half drunk on exhaustion?"

I stifle the urge to chuckle right then, pursing my lips together at the memory.

"One drink isn't going to take that long. And Oliver doesn't come back until tomorrow, so you still have lots of time to yourself, am I right?"

It's the time to myself that bothers me most. That's when I do too much thinking and worrying. That's when the memories take over, and I'm reminded of how lonely it is to be a single, widowed mom.

Maybe she's right, as horrible as that may be.

"One drink. Then you assholes leave me alone and let me leave in peace."

"Deal." Bethany wraps her arm around me. "Dale! Get this woman a drink!"

Deal. Why do I feel like the deal I just made is with the devil?

As Dale makes his way toward the bar, I stuff my hands in my pockets, feeling wildly out of place here. Bars used to be where Denny and I hung out all the time, before Oli was born. We practically lived at the piano bar downtown, but now they're crowded and loud, and far too stuffy for my comfort.

"Come sit here, Nola." Shay waves me over to an empty space between her and Simon, who looks about as out of place as I feel. By the time I take a seat, Dale's back, setting down a Long Island iced tea, evident in the gradient of browns and the lime stuck to the rim of the glass.

"You had to pick a drink with all kinds of alcohol?"

"If you're gonna have one, might as well make it a good one, right? *Enjoy.*" He takes a seat in the chair across from me, and lifts his bottle of beer for a toast before clinking the side of my glass.

Enjoy. I stare at the drink I used to love, back in my party days, trying to remember the last time I ordered one myself. Maybe six years ago. I take a sip, and my mouth is instantly delighted by the flavor, as if my taste buds have waited years for this moment. It's smooth, without the sting of all the alcohol I know goes into them. The sign of a talented bartender. Easing back into my seat, I watch Beth drag Shay out onto the dancefloor, and shake my head when she reaches back for me.

"Baby steps," I say after her.

"Fine. But I'm getting your ass on the dancefloor again soon. Mark my words, Tensley."

She and Shay hustle toward the jukebox, and I sip more of my drink.

"I don't get the need for attention," Simon says beside me. "It's a foreign concept to me."

"You're not the only one." I snort, using my straw to move around the large chunks of ice in my drink. "Give me a quiet night at home with a book, or a movie, and I'm in heaven."

"That's refreshing to hear. Feels like everyone I meet is some kind of ... party animal."

"Party animal or haughty little snob who won't give you the time of day," Dale adds before taking another swig of beer. "Believe me, I've tried." He pushes out of his chair, heading toward the bar again. Guy might end up having to remortgage his home after all, if he doesn't slow down.

Another sip of my drink, and I can feel my muscles growing warm, the room feeling less intimidating, bigger and lively. "Those days are gone for me. I'm just an old maid in dire need of a cat," I say to Simon, who still sits beside me.

My mind instantly flips to earlier in the evening, when Voss stood in the doorway, shirtless, holding the tiny kitten. How, for a split second, I almost wished I was that cat nuzzled into his chiseled chest.

"You like cats?"

I shrug and set the straw to my lips, noticing my drink is half gone already. *Slow down, Nola.* "The stuffed variety."

In my periphery, I catch Simon's head snapping in my direction, and I slap a hand to my mouth to keep from spewing my last sip, as I snort a laugh. "As in, my son's toys. I can't really deal with too many live things. Plants. Animals. Other people."

"Plants and animals aren't so bad. It's the people I have trouble with. Socializing doesn't really come natural for me."

"Me, either." Glancing to the side, I offer Simon a smile. "It's nice meeting a fellow hermit."

He lifts his glass, which looks to be a soft drink. "Cheers."

"Cheers," I echo, clinking my glass against his.

My head is spinning as I sit in the booth, squished between Simon and Shayna, who talk to each other through me, as if I'm not even here. Their words are a jumbled mess, bouncing around in my brain. I'm three drinks in and officially buzzing. Or maybe I'm trashed and just don't realize it yet.

My whole body feels warm and fuzzy, muscles completely relaxed.

Simon lifts his drink, wiping down the condensation left on the table with his napkin, and sips his Coke like it's Grand Marnier, or something.

I find the act mesmerizing, consuming my attention as though it's the most riveting thing I've seen, and it's not.

A hot, muscled man holding a kitten pretty much trumps everything.

And now I'm perving on my tenant again.

Without warning, I push to my feet, interrupting Simon and Shayna, and feel a gentle grip of my hand.

"Everything okay, Nola?" Simon asks, his face somewhat of a blur.

"Yeah … I just …" I stumble backward, the room spinning way too fast in my periphery. "I just need some air."

"Want me to come with you, hun?" Shay tips back the last of her beer and signals the waitress for another.

"No. No, I just need a minute to get some fresh air. You two stay. Talk."

Eyes focused on the exit sign ahead, I make my way toward it on legs that feel like wet noodles, until I finally push through to the back alley. The stench of the dumpster and stale water assault my nose, taunting my gag reflex, but I hold it back and fish through my coat pockets for my cigarettes. The buzz of nicotine only adds to my dizziness as I light up, and I don't immediately notice someone's joined me, until arms wrap tight around my torso.

"Found ya!" Harv stinks like the onion rings he was eating earlier, and I wrench his fingers apart to set me loose.

"Get off of me."

He does, laughing as he lights up one of his own cigarettes. "Shouldn't come out here by y'self." His words are slurred and forced. "Buncha freaks 'n this par'of th'city."

I may be buzzing myself, but even I can see he's straight up shitfaced, his eyes falling to half-mast as he wavers on his feet. "I'm fine."

"You are fine. And I wish y'were mine." The song in his voice stirs the bile I tried to hold down from before. He shakes his head, his right sleepy eye twitching. "Why'n't we jus' fuck? Jus' ge'it over and fuck already?"

"Because I have self-respect. And you have a wife."

"You're too good f'me? 'S'at it, Nolo?"

It's not even worth correcting him again, especially when he only butchers my name to piss me off.

Flicking my cigarette away, I take a step toward the door, but he blocks me. "I'm going back in now. Please get out of my way."

"Touch m'dick firs'." Thumb tucked in the waistband of his jeans, he holds his pants open in invitation. "Th'I'll let you back in."

"Fuck you." I step to the right, and when he follows suit, I quickly skirt to the left, but he catches me, even in his drunken state, pulling me into him.

Jeans still pulled away from his body, he tightens his grip around me and presses me against the wall. "C'mon, Lola. Touch m'dick. Jus' once. One little stroke."

Struggling against him, I push away, trying to create a wider gap for escape, but he has the advantage between his body and the wall. "Get the fuck off of me!"

"Y'know you want to touch. Jus' squeeze it, and I'll let y'go."

"Fuck off! Help!"

He abandons his waistband and slaps his hand over my mouth. "Shhhh. I'm jus' playin', baby. 'Sall fun." His lips only brush across my cheek, before his body is hefted backward, his grip faltering.

Standing beside me is Simon, brows angled to a pissed-off frown.

Wiping sweaty hands against my jeans, I straighten myself, dumbfounded for a moment, trying to process how someone as small as Simon managed to throw off someone as heavy as Harv.

"Th'fuck? Who th'fuck d'you think …?" Harv lurches again, but one solid punch to his stomach sends him stumbling back onto his ass. Idiot looks like a stuck turtle trying to turn himself over. "Whassa problem? I was jus' playin' wi' her."

"Are you okay?" Simon's eyes are warm and sympathetic, as if he's apologizing for all of the male species at once.

"Yeah. I'm … just a little … tipsy, is all."

"If you'd like, I can give you a ride home. I haven't consumed any alcohol tonight, just soda."

"Y'don't have to do that, Simon." I could call a cab, but that would cost money that I didn't bother to bring and can't really afford to blow.

"Would you prefer Shay drive you? I'll understand if you do. I just don't think you should drive yourself."

Shay's not much more sober than I am. And Dale has thrown back a few drinks, so I don't know if he's in any better shape. Simon is my best bet, and at least I know him slightly better than some random cab driver.

"You don't mind driving me?"

"Not at all. Let me grab my coat." He opens the door for

me, and I glance back toward the sounds of hurling, to find Harv bent forward, puking beside the dumpster.

Shaking my head, I head back into the bar and wave to Dale from the door. Head tipped like he's confused, he waves back, until I point to Simon, and Dale shakes his head, waving me over instead. Even when tipsy himself, the guy looks out for me. Through the crowd, I meet him halfway and catch the slight drunken sway when he stops before me.

"Where'ya goin'?" His brows are stern with concentration. Reminds me of my father when he'd get pissed at me for something.

"Simon's driving me home."

Eyes clamped, Dale shakes his head fervently. "Nah, that's ... lemme drive you home."

Not a chance. The guy has clearly had as much as everyone else. "Thanks Dale, but you should really get a ride yourself. I'm sure Simon would drive you, too."

He scoffs at that and glances away and back. "I'm fine. I'll take you home. I'll take care of you, Nola." He's not as drunk or obnoxious as Harv, but he's starting to make me just as uncomfortable.

"Really, I'm just ... just gonna catch a ride with Simon."

His eye twitches, as he stares down at me, and tips back another sip of beer, lips tight when he swallows it back. "Think that's a better idea?"

The back of my neck feels like it's on fire, as I clear my throat and drop my gaze from his. "Yeah. I do."

"Fine. Get a ride from Simon then," he says, and walks back toward the table with the others.

Perhaps the strangest encounter I've ever had with Dale, though it occurs to me it's the first time I've seen him intoxicated. Maybe I'm reading too much into it, in my own drunken state. He's always been overprotective of me, after all.

A nudge at my arm draws my attention toward Simon, who tips his head toward the door. With his coat in hand, he leads me out to the parking lot, toward a silver Malibu parked two cars down from my Jeep.

Practically leaping ahead of me, he rushes to open my door, and sets a hand on my shoulder, as I slide into his passenger seat. The car has a crisp, lemon scent, and I glance up to see a yellow air freshener dangling from the rearview, along with two air fresheners clipped to the vents.

Guy likes lemons.

He falls into the driver's seat and fires up the vehicle, turning the heater up. "Feel free to make it warmer, if you'd like. Kind of a chilly night."

"Simon, thank you for this. I know I don't talk to you much, but … I'm just … not a real sociable person."

"I understand. You, um … mentioned that earlier." His comment draws my mind to a vague conversation from earlier, and I rub my temples, my sudden embarrassment only adding to the warm flush of my cheeks.

He stops the vehicle at the entrance of the bar and waits. "Where to?"

"Newland Avenue. Know where that is?"

"I think so. I suppose, if I get lost, that's what GPS is for, right?"

I chuckle at that, setting my attention on the passing buildings, as he drives us toward my house. "Thanks for what you did back there. Harv is such a dick."

"He really is. But don't tell Bethany I said that."

"He makes my skin crawl. Guys like that are just …"

"It infuriates me to see a man treat a woman so … poorly. My mother suffered abuse from my father when I was a child. It's a … sensitive topic for me."

"My mother ignored my father. He did everything for her." It's the alcohol talking, because no way in hell I'd have admitted that aloud, otherwise. "I'm sorry, my mind is on autopilot right now."

"It's okay. I don't judge anyone."

"You're a nice guy, you know that? Don't ever change, because ... there just aren't enough nice men in the world, anymore."

"I don't plan on changing anytime soon."

Rubbing my forehead, I mentally tamp down the urge to cry over what happened in the alley, but the note pops into my head again, stirring anger, instead. "Harv ... he left a note on my car. Said ... would you rather be strangled, or raped?"

"Did you report it?"

"I should've, but not yet. I wanted to give him a chance to confess to it."

"Did he?"

"Of course not. Just like he was *only playin'* back in the alley."

"Somebody needs to set him straight. To show him how to treat a woman."

I huff staring down at my hands, folded in my lap. "Can I ask you something?"

"Of course."

"Do you have a thing for Bethany?"

"Bethany? No. Uh ... she's married."

"If you call it that. I mean, most married couples I know have vows."

Hands set at ten and two on the steering wheel, he shakes his head, eyebrows furrowed. "I don't mess with married women. It's not right."

"My house is the one on the right, ahead," I say, pointing through the windshield. "Well, if you ever decide to get married, you're going to make one hell of a husband." Patting him on the shoulder, I wait until he brings the car to a stop at the curb and set my hand on the door.

"I appreciate that. Would you like me to walk you to the door?"

"No, I got it from here. Thanks for the ride, Simon."

Lips tight, he gives a nod. "Anytime. Take care."

I exit the vehicle, proud of myself for being an adult and trusting someone to drive me home, when I sure as hell wouldn't have done such a hot job myself. Stumbling up to the front door, I turn to see he's still waiting at the curb, and it's only when I take a step inside the house that I see the car roll forward. With a wave, I close him out and peek through the peephole to see his car driving off down the street.

Well, that was ... *nice.*

As I turn away from the door, a thought hits me. I'll have to have someone drive me to get my Jeep tomorrow morning before I have to pick up Oli.

Shit.

9

THE SANDMAN

*O*ne week ago ...
The Loop was the perfect place to pick up a woman. Everyone was transient, looking for a party and a quick hookup. The streets were packed most evenings with young, twenty-and-thirty-something socialites, who made up most of the demographic. Loud, obnoxious girls who stumbled along from place to place, getting more intoxicated by the hour. *Insolent bitches in their fuck-me clothes.* Even in the winter months, they frequented the bars in slinky skirts and crop tops, or skimpy dresses that showed off their bodies.

Little whores craving attention.

And stupid, too.

Had they watched the news, they might've known not to parade around like drunken vermin, practically begging to be snatched up by a cunning predator. In the last year, three girls had gone missing from Chicago, their bodies discarded miles away, eyeballs removed and filled with sand, a signature that gave the killer his moniker: *The Sandman.*

A name that'd grown on him.

He sat at a small round table, where heaters kept the forty-degree chill off him, as he waited for the perfect subject. Most of the girls sported small breasts and tiny waists—practically birds without any real meat.

No, he liked the curves best, and big sloppy breasts that bounced when they moved. Made him hard just thinking about a woman lying sprawled out before him, eyes rolled back into her head.

Teeth gritting, he squeezed the napkin in his hand, willing away the disgust creeping up his throat at the visual.

A busty blonde squeezed through a crowd, not even sparing him a glance as she passed his table. Strange how human beings, the highest functioning organisms on the planet, with all their acute means of perception and cognizance, could be so blind to what lay in their periphery. The woman didn't seem to have any idea that she'd seen him before, just two nights back, in fact, when he'd followed her into a restaurant, where she met up with friends for dinner. She'd offered no more than a passing glance on her way to the loudest table there. Perhaps she had no idea that he'd watched her at work all week long, passed her on the street, as she hustled to grab a coffee before her staff meeting. That he'd witnessed her taking home a stranger from the bar the weekend before and fucking him in the backseat of his SUV before they'd even arrived.

She didn't seem to recall seeing the terrifying entity everyone called *The Sandman*, watching her every move for nearly two weeks. Because surely, if she had, she wouldn't have ventured out on the one-month anniversary of his previous kill. Unfortunately, the police wouldn't yet be privy to such a pattern, since the one before last had been dumped three months earlier. The one before that?

Six.

No, she was as flagrantly obtuse as the rest of them.

Nothing but a filthy young sow, whose only purpose in life was to breed more of her kind. As if he'd sit by and allow such a thing.

The Sandman lifted his glass from the table, using the balled up napkins to wipe where condensation had gathered. He tossed the used napkin into the overflowing trash bin on his way to where she stood checking her watch.

"Can I buy you a drink?" he asked, setting his glass on the bar beside her.

A quick once-over, and she feigned the kind of smile that set his teeth on edge. The kind that told others around them she was just being polite for face. He clearly wasn't her type, evident in the brawny rich men she'd often let fuck her like a bitch in heat.

That was the beauty of masks. Essentially, everyone wore them. All of them hiding what truly lay beneath all that makeup and mannerisms. If each person could be seen for what they were, she'd be just as ugly as he was.

"No, thank you. I'm just waiting for some friends." She didn't even bother to mention she'd seen him around. Why would she? Women like her only saw what they wanted to see. Everything else merely served as a prop. Nothing but background noise to their perfect little existence.

Of course she wasn't interested—whores like her only went for the beefy and dim-witted, the ignorant twits who got every piece of ass at The Loop because they spent most of their lives building their biceps instead of their brains. The ones who flaunted their money like a calling card for the equally rich and haughty.

The Sandman gave a nod and lifted his drink, grabbing another napkin to wipe the condensation left there.

His eye twitched with the thunderstorm of anger rolling through him, while he made his way toward the exit, tossing the glass and another balled up napkin into the trash. Not that he'd expected her to say anything different.

Dirty sluts rarely went for the highly-educated, much more worldly men.

Hands balling into tight fists, The Sandman made his way through the tightly woven crowd, knocking into a shoulder as he passed a group standing around.

A woman's cranberry colored drink splashed over the glass and she scowled back at him. "Hey! Watch where you're going!"

Like the response of a robot, her words spun him around, and his eyes locked on her short auburn trusses, neatly pulled back into a stunted ponytail. As he took a moment to assess her features, a larger male blocked his view.

"'The fuck you looking at, man?" Standing nearly a foot taller, the other male towered over The Sandman, and just like that, his interest in the woman waned. He turned back along his path, out of the bar, and down the street to the parking garage, where the blonde had parked earlier.

Where she parked every week, at around the same time, when she came out to have drinks with friends.

Slumped in the driver's seat of his own vehicle, he kept his eyes on the fancy Lexus sedan parked across from him. Hours passed, and he watched others come and go. He checked his watch. She'd be leaving soon, possibly with another man.

He'd taken that into account, as well.

Nabbing a leather case from beside him, he exited his vehicle, and looking around the dimly lit garage, so as not to be taken by surprise, he made his way to the Lexus. With gloved hands, he slipped a small piece of paper onto the windshield of the vehicle.

On the car door keypad, he punched the code he'd

watched her use a few times, when she'd mindlessly locked her keys inside, and crouched low in the backseat.

Waiting.

It wasn't long before the first sounds of her familiar voice reached his ears where he lay across the rear foot well.

"I'm good. Catch you guys next week! Randy, don't let that bitch drive. Way too many grapefruit crushes!"

A male responded with something incoherent, his voice growing distant.

The thump of her wipers told him she'd pulled the note from the windshield. Through the driver's window, he could see her looking around the garage, as if she might catch a glimpse of who'd left it. With the paper held to her face, he could see her eyes move back and forth, reading his proposition, and a smile stretched across his face when her brows pinched together. The note fluttered out of her hand, and she bent forward, the scratch of the door telling him her hands were unsteady, likely trembling, as she tried to fit the key.

Her hands slid over the keypad, instead, and the vehicle lock popped. Discarding her bag on the seat beside her, she fell into the driver's seat, the sound of her shaky breaths only goading his excitement. A strong, berry scent filled the car, gagging him where he lay. Floral scents were one thing, but sweet smells sickened him.

Shaky hands fumbled over the steering wheel to the ignition, in a futile attempt to start the car. To get away. Almost laughable, but he remained silent as he sat up and plunged the needle into her neck, watching her wide eyes droop with sleepiness while the tranquilizer took over. Gently cupping the side of her head, he lowered her across the console and stared down at her.

Blue eyes shifted back and forth, and warm pants of breath fanned his cheek.

If she could talk, she'd tell him *sorry*, for how she'd

treated him earlier. She'd beg for her life and to be spared out of mercy. She might even give him the answer to his question, unflinchingly choosing to fuck him.

But it was too late for all that. He already knew what mask he'd make her wear. How he'd tuck her hair inside of it, just so. The color crimson he'd paint on her lips.

She would be his doll, his plaything, to do with as he wished. She'd never reject him again.

He'd make her virtuous and obedient. Gracious as a flower.

His Queen of the Night flower.

And in the morning, she would wilt away.

Just like the others.

10

VOSS

I'm just stepping out of the shower when a knock at the door stops me in my tracks. After nabbing my gun from the nightstand, I slink toward the bedroom window and, peering out, see Nola at the front door, biting her nails. A quick scan of the yard and driveway confirms there's no one else, and I set my gun back where it was, before making my way to the door in nothing but a towel wrapped around my lower half.

Not that I mind the chick, , hell, she made a kids food-stained Star Wars T-shirt look like a wet dream, but I hope this isn't going to be the same routine every day. I'm here to watch and observe her, not play some friendly game of *Mister Rogers' Neighborhood.*

When I throw back the door, her eyeballs look as if they might pop out of her head. Decked out in a red flannel shirt, ripped up jeans, and Sherpa coat, with her hair twisted up in a red bandana, she looks like a woman who belongs in a cabin in the woods, on the cover of an *Outdoor Living* magazine.

Painfully attractive, in spite of being fully clothed.

"I'm ... sorry. I didn't mean to catch you off guard. Again." Head tilted away, it's obvious she's trying not to look at my towel. "My car is parked at the bar, and I just wondered if you could give me a ride. I have to pick up my son in an hour."

This is turning into exactly what I don't need. "I'm supposed to be somewhere this morning, too. What about a cab?"

"Look, I wouldn't ask, asking isn't something I do, but I made a mistake last night. One I don't intend to make again. If you can't give me a ride, I'm happy to walk. I just thought I'd try first."

"How far is the bar?"

"About five miles. Just up Grand Avenue. A straight shot."

"It'll take you an hour just to walk there." Striding back into the bedroom, I nab a fifty from my wallet and return to where she's still standing outside the door. "For a cab."

Brows furrowed, she stares down at the cash, and when her eyes find me again, they carry sadness, more than anything else. "Never mind. Thanks, anyway."

"What's the problem?"

"The problem is, that I decided to cut loose a little bit last night. Which is a first for me. But see, fate doesn't like when I do anything outside of busting my ass, so now I'm having to figure my shit out the next day." With a huff, she shakes her head. "It's not your problem, and I'm thoroughly embarrassed for having asked you. I'm sorry, you must think I'm some crazy helicopter landlord."

"I'm starting to wonder."

Her lips crack with a slight smirk, as her eyes shy away from mine. "Thanks for the offer. The cab. But it's not that far. Have a ... good day."

"Why don't you do yourself a favor and take the cash? It'll save you some time."

"Really, I'll just walk. I probably need to walk off this hangover, anyway. Thanks, though." Backing away from the door, she shuffles back down the stairs and off toward the sidewalk, like she's really going to make that five-mile hike to get her car.

Stubborn as fuck.

And the intrigue just keeps on with this girl.

It takes me about twenty-five minutes to get dressed and feed a small bit of tuna to the kitten I've named Vince. By the time I catch up with Nola, she's already a couple miles down Grand Avenue, and I slow my car along the curb, rolling the window down.

"C'mon, I'll give you a ride."

She glances toward me for a second. "I told you, I can walk. It's no big deal."

"Quit being stubborn. I don't have time for stubborn. Just get in the car."

"I know that. You don't have time. It's okay. Look, I wasn't putting this on you. Really, I wasn't."

"I get your MO. You don't ask for help. You asked me, and that was probably a big deal for you, so get in. I'm driving you." I stop the car alongside her. "I'm not going to ask again."

"Oh, yeah? What'll you do, instead? Chase me down and drag me into the car?"

"If absolutely necessary, yes."

"Fine." She rolls her shoulders back like she's brushing off her pride, then throws back the passenger door and slumps into the seat beside me. The way she mulishly crosses her arms beneath her breasts pushes them up toward the low dip of her flannel shirt.

I take off down the street, shaking my head. "I can't tell if you're brilliantly manipulative, or just pig-headed to a fault."

"Well, I'm still getting a feel for whether, or not, you're a closet serial killer, so I guess we're even."

"Did you call Jackson yet?"

"No. I was too busy dealing with a hangover and asking you for a ride. Both of which have only made my headache worse." She clutches her skull, sadly covering up the cleavage from a moment ago. "I haven't had a hangover since before Oliver was born."

"Bloody Mary. Make sure you get the good vodka. Not the cheap shit."

"I can't do Bloody Mary's. For one, they're gross. And … well, they're just gross."

"So, how did you get home last night? Drunken stumble of shame?"

"Someone *offered* to drive me. Which had me all believing in the goodwill of men when I woke up this morning. Must've still been drunk to ask you for help."

"And this Good Samaritan is a friend of yours?"

"He's been coming into the diner for a while. All the waitresses know him."

"All except you?"

"I never really talked to him much, until last night. But he seems like a nice guy. Which is a rarity these days."

"He's probably trying to screw you."

"Excuse me?"

"Is he an older guy? Younger guy?" My question is part curiosity, part ruling out a potential killer.

"Younger than me."

Too young to be my sadistic uncle then.

"If I was attracted to a woman, I'd play the nice guy angle, drive her home to find out where she lives. If he pops in to check on you, he's definitely trying to get you in the sack."

"Well, thanks for that … worldly advice, Voss. That's my car parked over there."

I turn into the lot of the Cobblestone bar and pull up behind the white Jeep. "Good luck today, *Star Wars*."

"Thanks for the ride," she says, clambering out of the passenger seat. "Good luck at your … meeting, or whatever you're doing."

The moment she reaches the Jeep, I steer the Audi toward the exit, waiting on the rush of traffic. In my rearview, I see her get into the car, and after a good thirty seconds, it still doesn't fire up, evident in the lack of smoke from the exhaust.

It's only when the traffic has passed, and I turn out onto the road, that I see her climb out of the Jeep, throwing her arms up into the air.

My guess is that her piece of shit car won't start.

'Fucks sake, this woman is one disaster after the next. Everything inside of me says it's not my problem. *She's* not my problem. After all, I didn't come here to play guardian angel to a woman who doesn't seem to have her shit together. I came to catch a deranged psychopath, who plans to add a new set of eyeballs to his collection.

And yet, without much prompting from my head, I turn the car back around and, parking alongside her, find her clutching the steering wheel and resting her forehead against it. There's something about her that I can't quite put my finger on. She's strong, but vulnerable in a way that doesn't come off as pathetic. It appeals to me, somehow. The tenacity of a woman who refuses to break, even when shit keeps weighing her down.

A sadist's wet dream.

The moment she catches sight of me, she turns her head, as if to keep me from seeing her, and wipes at her cheeks.

Leaning onto my elbow, I stroke my chin to bury the chuckle begging to escape. Not at her, but at the ridiculous nature of it all. If this were a cartoon, the vehicle would fall apart all around her, and she'd still be left stubbornly clutching that steering wheel. "What's the problem?"

"It's nothing, Voss. Really. I called my brother. They're just getting home from church, but he's going to come get me. So, you don't have to stay here."

"What's happening with the vehicle?"

"I tried to turn the key over, and it's not starting. I don't know what's wrong with it."

"Have you called a tow truck?"

"I'm waiting for my insurance to tell me if it's covered."

"And if it's not?"

"I'm just trying to take this one step at a time, so I don't lose my shit and end up in a straitjacket. But either way, I'll figure it out. So, just go."

"How about I give you the rent and security deposit we talked about, but never finalized. Three thousand, I think? You call a tow truck, a therapist, whatever you need to deal with the problem."

"It was only the security deposit and the first month's rent. Twenty five hundred."

"Well, I haven't yet gotten rid of the cat, so consider the extra a pet deposit."

"The cat is the least of my worries right now. If this ends up being the starter, I'm probably going to need a case of Xanax, more than anything."

"Well, before you get drug-happy, you need to get your car out of this lot." I reach into the glovebox and pull out my wallet, counting out ten hundred dollar bills that I hand off to her. "Here's a thousand. I'll transfer the additional two thousand. Can you receive cash payments to your phone?"

"Like, Apple pay? I think so."

I pull up her phone number and transfer the funds in a matter of a couple clicks. "Done. Now do whatever you need to do to get your son."

"Voss … I can't …. This isn't right."

I don't bother to tell her that my time is more valuable to me than the few extra bucks I've offered. That I'd much prefer to part with the cash, than sit and watch her ponder all the ways she can stubbornly refuse what I owe her anyway. I get a sense that Nola is the type who'd bleed out for someone and reject the tourniquet that'd save her from hemorrhaging to death. "Are you all set, then?"

Still teary-eyed, she swipes at her cheek again and nods. "Thank you for this."

There's a strange sensation humming through me when I stare back at her half-cocked smile and shiny eyes. A zap of something foreign and gratifying at the same time. The way one might look upon a small bird that has just eaten from the palm of his hand.

The very thought has my fingers curling into tight fists, just as they would with a bird so trusting.

With a nod, I throw the car in drive and attempt to get on with my day.

Goodwill of men.

Bullshit.

The Royal Roadway motel has to be the seediest joint in Chicago, located at the intersection of Jackson Boulevard and Highway 50. The kind of place that takes cash and rents by the hour. Scanning my surroundings, I stride up to the room number that's written on the inside flap of the matches and check the door. Peering through the narrow gap in the curtains shows an empty room inside, bed made as if it hasn't been slept in, at all. A *Do Not Disturb* sign dangles from the doorknob, which I attempt to turn.

Locked.

The maid cart, two rooms down, draws me to where an older woman, maybe sixty, gathers up sheets from the room's unmade bed.

"Excuse me," I say, interrupting her cleaning.

She swings around, frowning. "Can I help you?"

"I left something in my room. Locked myself out. Just wondering if you could let me back in?"

"I'm sorry, you'll have to get a key from the office."

Tugging the fifty from my pocket, I flash it in front of her. "It'll take only a minute."

Lips tightened, she huffs and hobbles toward me, swiping the proffered money on the way, and leads me back toward the other door. Two seconds later, I have full access to the room and don't waste any time in my search. Under the bed. In the nightstand. The maid stands in the doorway the whole time, watching me. It's not until I reach the bathroom that I find what I'm looking for. Set out on the counter is a cheap men's watch. I lift it from the sink, examining it for any sign that it might be the ignition switch for an explosive, or something. On the back, etched in its gold plating: *To the moon and back* is all that's written.

I don't have time to disassemble the thing here, to make sure there's no tracking device inside, so I stuff it in my pocket and offer a smile as I pass the maid. "Thank you," I tell her on the way out.

"No problem."

Once inside my car, I remove a small pocket knife from the glovebox and pop the back cover that holds the dedication. The likelihood of something being small enough to attach inside is slim, but I don't take any chances. Nothing but gears. After replacing the back, I stuff it into the console beside me and fire up the vehicle. I don't leave, though. Instead, I park a few lots over, alongside the curb, where the door to the motel remains in view, and I wait.

Ten, twenty, thirty minutes pass with no disturbance.

When a thought strikes me, I exit the vehicle, pulling a pack of smokes from my pocket as I do so, and I pretend to drop my lighter, elated when it falls beneath the car. I steal a moment to make a quick sweep of the undercarriage and find a small black device attached there.

A tracker.

Bastard must've watched me enter the room and planted it then. No doubt, he's watching me now, so I leave it in place, retrieving my lighter, instead, and keeping on with my ruse by taking a few quick puffs of my cigarette.

"Good one, asshole. But not good enough."

If it were me, I'd have taken a shot already, but I know that's not how he works. Carl doesn't want fast and easy. He wants me to play his game until the end, drawing each moment out with the same agony with which he torments his victims. Having been one once, I know this about him. Unfortunately for him, I've come to enjoy games just as much.

I click an app on my phone, one designed by a friend of mine I met in the military, who went on to study at MIT. He provided me with the VPN app I use to conceal my IP address, but it also contains a GPS spoofer.

The first step is to jam his tracker, which will merely look like a delay in movement.

With the phone set out on the seat beside me, I leave the parking lot and head toward the nearest mall, keeping an eye on the traffic in my rearview, in case anyone is following behind.

Choosing a crowded part of the mall's lot, I steal the last spot between two large SUV's, then make my way into the mall. Once inside, I pop in to the nearest rest room and set the spoofer's location to the Jansen estate, my old house, about ten miles north—only address I can think of off the top of my head. After a good five minutes, I execute it, before taking my time walking back to my car.

The dot on his tracker should've set back into motion and will appear like I'm on my way toward the old house. I am, but not before he gets there first.

A block up the street from the Jansen estate, I wait inside my idling car for a vehicle to arrive. Two minutes later, a white panel van pulls up in front of the house and sits in the driveway.

I snap a quick pic of the license plate.

Instead of climbing out of the vehicle, though, the driver backs out of the drive, and I miss the opportunity to plant the tracker back on him.

Fuck.

He takes off the way he arrived, and as I pass the house, following after him, I toss the tracker out the window.

Keeping about five car lengths behind, I follow him through the streets, until we reach a place called Duli's Diner —the same diner noted in Nola's progress notes by her psychiatrist.

Parked across the street, I watch him clamber out of the van, his face concealed by a black hoodie. Minutes later, a couple exits the diner. They don't even register on my radar at first, since the guy is taller and isn't wearing a hoodie, until the two of them jump into the same damn panel van. Suddenly, my *what the fuck* sensors go off.

Where the hell did hoodie go? And who the hell is this couple now?

The two drive out of the diner parking lot, leaving me to decide which one to go after. Dude in the hoodie is still in there, and he's the one I've been chasing this whole time.

Instead of following after the couple, I make my way across the street and enter the diner, scanning over the handful of people inside. Not a single one wearing a hoodie.

The guy in the booth across from me gives me a once-over, his burger halfway to his mouth.

"You seen a guy come through here wearing a hoodie?" I ask him.

He hikes a thumb over his shoulder and gives a nod. "Think he went out the back door."

With quick strides, I make my way down the adjacent hall, where the bathroom and kitchen doors line the corridor. At the end of the hall stands an exit, but the squeal of tires from behind has me spinning around, and I race back to the front of the diner.

Before I get a chance to see the vehicle, it disappears out of the lot.

"Fuck!"

The older couple sitting in the booth nearest to me look up with a shocked expression, but instead of offering an apology, I slam through the door.

Lost again.

11

NOLA

I stare down at the cash that fills my purse. One thousand dollars. Another two thousand sits in a wallet on my phone. In seconds, Voss turned my world from impossible, to what every white collar in the world must feel like. How liberating it must be to deal with issues so quickly and efficiently that they hardly make so much as a hiccup in the day. That's what I imagine Voss's life must be like. If something is broken, he has the means to fix it. When he wants something, he has the means to get it.

I sign the paperwork for the tow and hand over a hundred-dollar bill, waiting on the change. Hell, when was the last time I waited on change, instead of counting out pennies to meet the required charge?

The garage is going to keep the car and have offered me a rental in exchange, and a shiny red Explorer pulls up to the front of the building. The driver from the rental place conveniently located next door tosses me the key. "All set."

All set.

The only reason any of this is *all set* is because of Voss. Had he not given me the cash, I'd probably be scrambling to figure out how the hell to pay for everything, because apparently my insurance doesn't cover rental.

I drive the new car, which rides like a dream, to Jonah's house, and smile when Oliver walks up with a confused look on his face. "Hey, Champ, how ya like my new wheels?"

His brows furrow deeper, and I chuckle.

"Just a rental. The Jeep took a shit, so I have to drive this until it's fixed. Hop in."

Jonah strolls up behind him, holding a mug that says *Not all heroes wear capes*. "Everything work out with the Jeep? I'd have come picked you up, you know."

"Everything is great. Voss helped me out."

"Voss, huh?" Eye squinting, he takes a sip of coffee. "So, how is the new roommate?"

Oliver's head snaps in my direction, and I catch Jonah's flinch.

"Sorry. I forgot he hasn't heard the news yet."

Licking my lips, which suddenly feel as dry as cotton, I scratch the nape of my neck and smile back at Oliver, unsure of how he'll feel about another man in the house. I meant to tell him and introduce him to Voss. Eventually. "So ... there's a guy. He's going to be living in the apartment behind the house."

Oliver's pale blue eyes glower with the kind of anger that could peel the paint right off the walls, and when he directs his attention toward the windshield, crossing his arms, it's a sure sign he isn't thrilled with the idea.

"It's only for a month, Oli. And we'll have some extra cash. In fact, I was thinking we could order some pizza tonight. How's that sound?" I haven't ordered a pizza in months, thanks to being flat ass broke after groceries and bills.

"Um. Diane ... she ordered pizza the other night."

There's a sheepish quality to Jonah's voice, as if he still feels bad for ruining the surprise. "Sorry, Nola."

"No. No, that's fine. Maybe I'll make dinner tonight. Something good that you used to like as a kid." I ruffle his hair and force a smile. "You still like spaghetti, right?"

Eyes sliding to the side, Oliver nods and unravels his arms.

"Good. Spaghetti, it is!" Twisting the key, I fire up the Explorer, trying not to let Jonah see the look of relief on my face. He'd tell me that I don't have to try so hard to make Oliver happy all the time, that everything I do is enough, but Jonah doesn't know what it's like to go to bed every night feeling like it isn't. He doesn't understand that a parent's worst fear is watching a child try to deal and silently process the brutal and unforgiving nature of some human beings.

I try to put myself in Oliver's shoes every day, and it makes me angry, too. The betrayal, the fear, the untimely annihilation of innocence.

And I can't reverse it for him. I can't fix it or undo what's already been done. All I can do is pave the way to something brighter, less dark. To preserve those small bits of innocence from his past and let him reconnect with the carefree boy he once was. So, if that means making spaghetti for him tonight, that's what I'm going to do.

"Thanks again, Jonah. Tell Diane she's my rock star."

"Will do." Hand reaching through the window, he tugs me forward and plants a kiss on my forehead, then reaches out to give Oli a handshake. "Love you."

"Love you, too."

The moment we walk through the door, Oliver dumps his duffle bag at the entrance and runs up the staircase, probably to his bedroom. With a sigh, I lift the bag that's decorated in *Minecraft* characters up from the floor and set it out of the way. "Glad to have you home, buddy."

The doorbell rings, and a quick peek through the peephole shows Simon standing on my front porch. I snort at the sight of him, recalling Voss's words from earlier, and open the door.

"Hey, Nola. I, um … just came by to check you out. I mean, check on you."

"I appreciate that, Simon. I'm good today. Just a minor hangover, is all."

"Good. Okay, well, have a nice day, Nola."

Slapped with confusion, I tilt my head, watching him trot down the stairs like he's seriously leaving already. It's so ridiculous, I have to stifle the urge to laugh. "Simon! Um … do you … want a cup of coffee, or something?"

"No, no. I don't want to trouble you. I just wanted to check and make sure you didn't pass out and crack your head on something."

"It's coffee, Simon. No trouble."

"Maybe just one. And then I'll go. I have lots of errands to run today."

"Sure." I step aside, allowing him into the house, and direct him toward the kitchen. "Let me just fire up the Caffeine Machine, as I call it." My dad went all out a year into his retirement and bought a crazy expensive cappuccino/coffee/espresso machine. The thing is about ten years old, but still chugs away like a champ. "What's your poison?"

"Pardon?"

"What do you take in your coffee?"

"Just black, thank you."

114

I shiver at that, my jaw tingling with the memory of trying it once. It takes a special breed to drink black coffee, I'm convinced. "So, how is your day going?"

"Very well, thanks for asking. I'm glad to know yours is better today."

"It is." After setting the coffees on the table, I sit down across from him, and push a box of lemon cookies left out from breakfast earlier, toward him. "These are great with coffee. Try one."

He reaches toward the box, and in doing so, knocks his mug to the side. Steaming coffee splashes over the edge of the table, and when Simon startles out of his chair, a dark circle marks the spot on his thigh that captured the hot fluids.

"Oh shit!" I scramble forward, setting the cup upright and spin around for a towel. "Are you okay?" With the rag dangling from my fingertips, I hesitate to dry the spot too close to his crotch.

As if taking the cue, he nabs the towel and sets it there himself. "Yes, I um … can I use your bathroom?"

"Sure. It's just … down the hall. There are more rags under the sink if you need them," I say, tearing off some paper towel to sop the spilled coffee. Once it's cleaned, I toss the saturated scraps into the trash and plop back into my chair.

A minute later, Oliver enters the kitchen, removing his earbud, which blasts his music loud enough for me to hear, as he passes on his way to the fridge. He grabs a carton of orange juice from inside, while, eyes on me, he kicks it back without a glass, and I set my coffee on the table, frowning.

"Hey, manners. Get a glass." I know he's testing me. The therapist told me he probably would, and not to relent, or let him *control the situation*, as she put it.

Rolling his eyes, he sets the carton of juice back in the fridge and grabs a soda, instead.

"Half. And pour it into a glass. You don't need to consume an entire can of soda in one sitting."

As he nabs a glass from the cupboard, I catch his gaze skim toward the second coffee cup still set out on the table.

"A friend of mine stopped by. Someone from work. Would you like to meet him?"

Lip curled as though he's disgusted with the thought, he finishes pouring his Coke and leaves the can on the counter, before he exits the kitchen, stuffing his earbud back in.

I like to think I have infinite patience, but I also thought I'd have a few years before the bratitude reared its ugly face. Part of me tries to cut him some slack, but the momma in me, the one who used to be good at being a momma, anyway, says what he's been through doesn't give him the right to behave with such disrespect.

The second Oliver leaves, Simon returns wearing a large wet circle on his thigh, his face still red, as if he's embarrassed over spilled coffee.

"I should probably go."

"Simon, I've had to clean up far worse than a little coffee. That's pretty much the norm at a diner."

"I suppose I'm somewhat particular about my clothes."

"I'd stay away from parenthood, then. Especially boys. I swear, Oliver must've stained every outfit I put on him. Food, dirt, snot trails he'd wipe on his sleeve. Now *that* was gross having to clean."

Lips forming a hard line, he nods. "Well, I'll take that into consideration if I ever decide to settle down. Thanks for the coffee, Nola. I'm going to let you get on with your day."

The heavy thunder of music pounds overhead, and both of us look up toward the ceiling. Lips tightened, I offer a sheepish smile, as My Chemical Romance blares from Oliver's room. I only know the name of the band because I Googled the lyrics last week.

"I'm sorry. My son ... he's taken a liking to goth music, as of late."

"How old is he?"

"Just turned eleven a few months back."

"Wow, that's pretty dark for an eleven-year-old."

"Yeah. I know. I'm ... addressing it. Slowly."

"I knew goth kids in high school. Kinda strange."

"Well, in his defense, the last few months have been kinda rough on him. His dad died. In front of him."

Face etched with concern, he rubs his knuckles against his jawline. "Oh. I'm so sorry to hear that. I didn't realize ... I knew you'd been married, but I thought it was divorce. I'm sorry."

"It's been a tough road, but we're getting through it. Anyway, I appreciate you stopping in to check on me. That was nice." And nice that he didn't try to make a move on me.

"Of course. Say, Nola. Would you... would you want ... I mean, you can say no. But I wondered if you might want to have dinner with me, sometime?"

"Oh." Shit. It's not that Simon wouldn't be date material. Looks-wise, he's nothing special, but he seems nice enough. A little too young for me—I'm guessing by five, or six, years. Unfortunately, I'm in no place financially, or mentally, to jump into a romance with someone right now. "It might be a bit too ... soon. For me."

The red flare of his cheeks intensifies, and he takes a step back, dropping his gaze from mine. "Sure. Forget I asked. I'm sorry. I shouldn't have asked. Thanks again." Spinning on his heel, he makes a beeline for the front door, and I trail after him.

"Simon, wait! I'm sorry if that came off wrong." My words fail to slow him down, and he pushes through the front door. "Simon!"

Once outside, he twists to face me, staring at me through the storm door. "It's okay, okay?"

"Okay." Dumbfounded, I watch him stumble on his way down the stairs and hobble off to his car.

Once inside his car, he backs toward the end of the drive, and comes to an abrupt stop at the sound of a horn. Voss's black Audi backs up a little, allowing Simon to slip out, and as the black car crawls up the drive, I see Simon's car sitting just on the other side of it, as if he's waiting for something. He drives off down the street, and the bass from Oliver's room upstairs draws me back to the realization that I have some shit to address with my son.

Before that, though, I race out the back door, catching Voss before he enters his apartment, carrying what looks like a grocery bag.

"Hey!" I shout up to him, and he pauses to face me. Maybe it's the light hitting his face, or the angle from which he's looking down on me, but something about him is strikingly attractive. Which is thoroughly irritating, because no way do I need to be attracted to the first renter who comes along. And I'd hate to think it was money that made a man handsome in my eyes, but in all fairness, it's been a while since one handed over a wad of it all at once. "Thanks for your help today. I'd really like to do something nice in return and invite you to dinner with Oliver and me."

"It's no problem, *Star Wars*. But I'll take a raincheck on dinner."

"Oh." Not that I had any ulterior motives—really—but I suddenly feel the need to make the same exit that Simon did just moments before. And I kind of hate that he still calls me *Star Wars*. "Okay that's no problem. I just ... really appreciated what you did and wanted to return the favor."

"Consider your gratitude well-received."

"Oh. 'Kay. Cool. Well, that's all I wanted to say."

"Who was that? Pulling out of the drive when I arrived?"

"A friend. From work."

"What's his name?"

At the crack of a grin on his face, I frown. "Why do you ask?"

"He's the one who drove you home the other night?"

"Yes."

Snorting, he shakes his head and pushes the apartment door open. "I wasn't wrong."

"Um, if you're implying I just *bedded* him, you're dead wrong."

"Then, he didn't ask you to dinner?"

"He did. But it doesn't mean I accepted. Not that any of this is your business."

"You're right. It's not. And I don't care to make it my business. Have a good night, Nola."

The door closes, as if he's slammed it in my face, and I set my hands on my hips, shaking my head. "What the hell is it with this guy?"

VOSS

Vince, the kitten I should've let go by now, climbs up my pant leg, when I enter the apartment. I offload a bag filled with some dinner options, a couple bottles of wine, and a fifth of bourbon onto the counter. "C'mon, man, give me a minute to walk in the door."

My phone rings, and I answer the much-anticipated call from Jackson. "What do you got?"

"The van belongs to a Harvey Bennington. I'm forwarding his address to you. The guy has a couple of minor charges on his record, but nothing more than some pot possession and a sexual harassment complaint filed a few years back. The woman with him was likely Bethany Bennington, his wife. She works at the diner. Got picked up for prostitution at the age of twenty-five, and was admitted to an outpatient drug rehab center."

"The sexual harassment accusation. Where was this?"

"Nevada. Looks like Harvey lived there for a couple years, before moving to Chicago. One of his coworkers claimed he cornered her in the women's bathroom, trying to get her phone number."

"No other complaints? Nothing in the Chicago area?"

"None that I can see."

I doubt my uncle would have taken up with any accomplices, since he always thought of others as inferior to his intelligence. A Bonnie & Clyde duo just seems too messy, too sloppy, for someone as meticulous as he was. "All right, thanks for the information. And by the way, if you get a call from a woman named Nola, drop the creepy coworker act. Just be normal."

"What creepy coworker act?"

"The one where you tell them I drink tea with the old ladies at the local nursing home, and that you strive to be like me when you're forty."

"Too much?"

"I'm thirty-five, asshole. And I fucking hate tea. Do you know how much tea I've had to drink, thanks to you?"

"I'll go easy on the Boy Scout shit."

"Thanks. I'll be in touch."

Clicking off the call, I pry Vince from my leg, where he's been hanging out the whole time, and scratch behind his ears. "You know, for a little shit, you sure like to leave your marks."

I pour a glass of bourbon and deposit Vince onto the arm of the couch on the way to my bedroom. Once there, I catch sight of Nola through the window, in her kitchen, hair pulled back, towel tucked into her jeans beneath that flannel shirt. I take a sip of my drink, swallowing back the burn as it slides down my throat. My mind slips into visuals of sliding that towel over her mouth, gathering it in a tight fist at the back of her head, like a set of reins. Before I even realize it, I'm grinding my teeth while those thoughts somehow mingle with the puzzles already consuming my mind.

Perhaps the link between Harvey Bennington and my uncle can be made much faster than trying to piece it together myself. Might just take a little charm, something I've tried to keep flipped off around Nola, to avoid any unwanted chemistry between us. Chances are, she knows Bethany pretty well, though, which may prove helpful in tracking down Carl.

B ottle of wine in hand, I knock on the back door of the house, ears piqued to the music bleeding through. Rap, from the sound of the bass and rhythm of the lyrics.

No answer.

Another knock.

Nothing.

I turn the knob that's surprisingly *not* locked, and step inside, recognizing the song as one of Eminem's with an undertone of a female voice trying to keep up. Padding quietly down the hall, I listen out, and round the corner to find Nola with her back to me, half dancing, half rapping, as she stands at the stove, stirring what I have to believe is spaghetti sauce from the smell of it.

Bottle dangling from my hand, I cross my arms, leaning against the doorframe, and bite back the laugh itching to break free at the sight of her.

In a matter of seconds, she's into it, shaking her ass as she rattles off a string of lyrics with the articulation of a woman high on a shot of Novocain. Mumbling through half of them.

Running my tongue over my teeth fails to curb the sudden need to bite the shit out of something, as I watch her roll her hips to the music.

Ladle in hand, she spins around, and slams to a halt mid-twirl with a squeal. Sauce drips onto the floor, just before the ladle falls out of her hand.

"Oh, my God! You scared the shit out of me!" she says, clutching at her chest.

"Do you always sound like that when you rap?" Giving her a hard time has quickly made my list of simple joys, and I smile when her cheeks turn three shades of red.

"Like what?"

"Like someone wired your jaw shut."

"Do you ever knock before waltzing into people's homes?"

"I did knock. Multiple times."

"How'd you get in?"

"Turned the knob."

She rolls her shoulders back, seemingly embarrassed. "I must've forgotten to lock it after I invited you for dinner and you slapped me with rejection."

"Well, I changed my mind. Spaghetti sounds good."

A smile lights up her stunning brown eyes set beneath long lashes that curl upward. Paired with the dimple in her cheeks, she has that girl-next-door look down, assuming the girl-next-door looks like an innocent, exotic beauty. "In that case, let's eat!"

It's been a long time since I sat down at a proper dinner table, and I'd be lying if I said I wasn't just a bit unnerved by it. The last time was in New York, just before I put a bullet through my host's skull. Even that stirred less tension.

"You're not eating, Oli?" Nola asks her son, before shoveling a forkful of wound up spaghetti noodles into her mouth.

Of course not. Kid's eyes are glued on me at the moment,

have been ever since I sat down to eat. Thought he was mentally handicapped at first, but I guess that's not the case. It's not his stare that's got me edgy, though. Shit, I wear hostility like a second skin.

It's the way we look like a nuclear family gathered around the table, as if any of this is normal.

I catch the subtle shake of his head in my periphery, as I wind my fork against a spoon and chomp another bite.

"Stop staring. It's rude." The chide in her voice comes off clipped and muffled, like she's got her jaw locked.

"No. It's okay." Gaze focused on the task of spooling another bite of noodles, I offer only a slight smile. "Staring is an act of dominance. Challenge. Some believe you can reach an altered state of consciousness by staring for long periods of time. Most consider it a form of aggression. A battle of wills, so to speak." Resting my hands at the edge of my plate, I lift my gaze to his in an unwavering game of look away. "Do you feel in control right now, Oliver?"

The twitch of his right eye tells me he's uncomfortable. I catch the increased rise and fall of his chest, as his breaths scramble to meet his rapidly rising heartrate. Mine remains calm, steady, unruffled by his little act of power. The contest goes on, and without breaking my stare, I take another bite of spaghetti, keeping my eyes locked on his.

Only seconds later, the kid's brows take a sharp dive into the frown, pinching his face, and he kicks back from the table, sloshing wine over the rim of the glasses.

"Oliver Daniel Tensley!" Nola's voice fails to make a dent in the kid's pissed-off mask of aggression, and he curls his lip before running out of the room.

I trail my gaze after him, still keeping with the game, even as he tromps up the stairs.

With a huff of obvious frustration, Nola cups her face, then runs her hands through those long, chestnut locks.

"This will be the second time today I've had to apologize on his behalf."

"Why doesn't he talk?"

"Long story, Voss. *Long* story. And no happy ending, I'm afraid." She tips back her glass of wine and sets it over the purplish stain on the tablecloth.

"You've got three-quarters left in that bottle. I'd say you've got time."

Cheek dimpled with a half-cocked smile, she reaches for the bottle that's between us and pours another glass. "It's not something most people want to hear. I'm certain it's not something you want to hear."

"Why's that?"

She sits quietly for a moment, as though contemplating her response.

I like this about Nola, the way she considers her words, chewing on them before she spits them out.

"People tend to perceive the world as inherently good."

"But you don't believe that."

"I believe in balance. Yin and yang. Positive and negative energy. For all the good, there's an equal amount of bad to keep the universe in check. And if that's the case, there must be a whole lot of good somewhere in the world. Just isn't here."

"Somebody hurt your son."

Clearing her throat, she lifts her glass to her lips, pausing before she takes a sip. "Not directly, from what I can gather. But those are the worst scars, right? The ones you don't see."

She brushes her knuckles across her cheek and jawline, and I watch, fascinated by the beauty in her sadness. The way her eyes carry desolation, the same way a painting captures a single moment in time. "He watched his father brutally murdered by some meth-head. Some ... *junkie* who valued money and drugs over human life. Who had no idea a little boy watched on while his whole world caved in on him." The shine in her eyes fails to dull as she blinks at the tears gathering in them. "It's a shitty thing when a child is forced to hand over his innocence, that magic of childhood."

Her comment tugs at the dark cluster of thoughts sequestered in the back of my mind. Ones I refuse to entertain at the moment. "You're right. Those are the worst scars. The invisible ones."

Lowering her gaze, she sits quietly, and the way her eyes shift only slightly, it's as if a thousand thoughts are passing behind them. An observation that leaves me curious to know what this woman has been through in life that she can speak so matter-of-factly about pain, like a scarf she puts on when it's cold. The murder of a husband is tragic enough, and I've watched plenty of women try to piece life together afterward and fail to achieve any level of normalcy. But I get a sense that pain is home for Nola, just as it once was for me.

Without warning, she pushes up from the table and reaches for her son's untouched plate of food, stacking it on top of hers. As she flicks her fingers for mine, I gently brush her hand aside and push to a stand across from her.

"I'll help with dishes."

She rears back her head with a guarded smile. "Well, that's unexpected. Most of the men I know would sell off a kidney to keep from helping with the dishes."

"I suppose I value my organs a bit more than that."

Following her into the kitchen, I try not to stare at her round ass filling those tight jeans, but I find it impossible to look away from things that stir my imagination so vividly. The thought of how symmetrical it'd look with her straddling my leather barrel horse back at home.

Standing beside her as she fills the sink with soapy water, I glance over at the unused dishwasher.

"Sorry, it's broken. Haven't gotten it fixed yet." She sets

what clearly looks like handmade dishes, based on their differing sizes and slightly off colors, into the basin. One of the plates slips from her hand, landing on the sink divider with a clash. The plate cracks in half—one falling into the soapy water, the other into the rinsing basin. I lift the non-submerged one out of the sink and turn to toss it in the trash, when I feel a tight grip of my arm.

"No, wait." Taking the broken plate in hand, she runs her finger over the edge of the break. "It's clean."

"You're gluing it?"

"Um, something like that. It's called Kintsugi. My mother taught me the technique." At what must be a look of confusion on my face, she glances up and smiles. "My mother believed that everything had a lifeline, so to speak. A history. Even this plate. And to honor it, she would seal the pieces with gold." She sets the plate halves onto the counter and opens the cupboard, reaching for a bowl set off from the others stacked inside. A map of gold lines decorates the outer and inner surface of it, some very thin, others thicker, creating a beautiful webbing across the black glaze. "My mother ate oatmeal out of this bowl every single morning when she was alive. Her shakes were so bad, she must've dropped the damn thing and broke it a dozen times over the years. The morning I found her, though, the bowl was lying on the floor beside her, perfectly intact, in spite of the oatmeal splashed everywhere. The cracks had made it so strong, it didn't break the last time she used it."

I stare down at the bowl, the business half of my brain wanting to reject the poetry that breathes inside this woman. The other half of me is intrigued by her, so much so, I gently set the bowl back onto the shelf and grab a towel.

For the next twenty minutes, we wash the dishes, the pans and the countertops through benign conversation about her grandmother, who traveled the world and spent a good chunk of her youth in Japan. She apparently left the love of her life there and returned to the States to raise Nola's mother alone.

"So, that'd make you about a quarter Japanese?"

"Something like that. My dad was Swedish, so all the Scandinavian has kind of taken over."

Now that she says it, though, I can see it in her—the almond shape of her eyes that pairs beautifully with the chestnut brown, and the very pale tan of her skin that holds a soft peachy glow.

"I'm going to have another glass of wine," she says. "Want to join me?"

It's a risk, spending so much time with her, but one I'm willing to take for the sake of gathering as much as I can on Harvey and Bethany.

"Yeah, sure."

Back in the dining room, she plops down on the same chair as before, and I follow suit, taking my seat across from her. She kicks her legs up onto the table, and her long slender feet covered in thin socks leaves me to wonder how they'd look slung over my shoulders, digging into my back.

The raising of her glass to her lips draws me out of those thoughts. "The wine is good," she says before taking a sip.

"The food was better."

"Dale's special sauce. I agreed to stay an extra hour at the diner last week, in exchange for his secret recipe."

"Did you specifically *ask* for his special sauce in that exchange? Because I'm thinking you got shafted."

"No, I—" Her eyes narrow on me as the pun dawns on her. Slowly. "Very funny."

"Couldn't resist. You've worked there a while now?"

"A few years."

"How is it?" The conversation feels as normal as any, except it's not. This is the boring shit I have to weed through to get to the information I need. Who the hell would love a waitressing job? Woman probably busts her ass all day, for a bunch of ungrateful bastards who don't even tip the standard.

"How is it? As opposed to what? The hustle and bustle of Wall Street?" Her brows wing up while she pours more of the wine. "Exciting, let me tell you."

"Tell me."

"Oh, let's see. There's Dale, my boss, who you so grossly assumed was some kind of booty call. He's not, by the way. I'm pretty sure his favorite phrases are *'Order up!'* and *'Can you work this weekend?'*"

I bury a smile behind my own glass of wine.

"Then there are the customers. Always entertaining, especially when they're bitching about the food." Another long swill of her drink, and she tips the bottle for more.

I want to shake my head, knowing what's coming, and save her the embarrassment of another drunken night, but that won't get me the details I'm desiring more so than the preservation of her dignity.

"Shitty food, then?" I tease, surprised at how much I enjoy these kinds of interactions with her, and the way her face scrunches to a scowl every time, just before she's about to slap a retort.

"Seriously? You just raved about dinner, man. No, the food is great. The customers are just picky as hell. And how can I forget my coworkers? Particularly Bethany, who's always a trip."

"Bethany," I echo.

Ding ding ding.

"Yeah. She's married to Harv, who is another story, but regardless, she'd have a guy like you unwrapped, like a kid on Christmas morning."

I snort at that and lean back into my chair, watching the

wine commandeer this woman's usually tight-lipped confessions like truth serum. "Unwrapped?"

"She's a narco. No, wait. That's not the word I'm looking for. I mean nympho! She's a nympho and hits on any guy with a nice body."

"Like mine?"

"Yes. I mean, no! Yes, she'd hit on you, but don't trick me into saying you have a nice body, okay? That's rude."

There are four stages to drunkenness: the attempt to fake sobriety, quickly smothered by the string of truths that tend to fly out a drunk's mouth, until we arrive at slurring, and she's one step away from that, from what I can see. The final stage is passing out.

Rubbing my hand across my jaw is a poor attempt to hide my amusement.

"And Harv is the physical embodiment of every woman's nightmare, wrapped up in a beer gut. They're like ... perfect together."

"He sounds like quite a catch for her."

"Doesn't matter. They're swingers. Even if he doesn't get her hot to trot, someone else surely will." Her words have begun to slur a bit, as she prattles on about her friend. Feeding me random minutiae that hasn't yet clicked into place.

"I take it you don't care for the husband."

"That's putting it mildly."

The glass tips back again, and she's already polished off her third glass of wine in less than thirty minutes. My guess is, she'll be nursing another hangover at this rate.

"What bugs you about him?"

The way she holds her breath, brows pinched together, I know she's thinking. Of what, I can't be certain, but as the pinch grows tighter, so does the urge to sweep her up out of that chair and pin her to the wall behind her, while I fuck the truth out of her.

"Karma," she finally answers.

"Karma bugs you?"

"No. I mean, yes. It does. Which is why I'm not going to talk about them. I didn't mean to invite you over just to bore you with my freakish life."

"Your freakish life is far from boring."

The giggle that flies from her mouth is quickly capped by the slap of her hand, and the hiccup that follows is a sure bet the alcohol has kicked in.

"I don' need any more bad karma, right?"

"Having an opinion doesn't make for bad karma."

"No, but sharing it does."

"Touché." I smile back at her, catching the slight sway of her posture. "What's your opinion of me, *Star Wars*? Still think I'm a killer?"

"I'm still formin' my opinion, but if y'are, you've got great taste in wine!" She lifts her glass like a toast and tips back the last sip in the glass.

"Drink it up."

"I will, thanks. Wait. You didn't poison it, did you?"

I feign a glance at my watch and smile. "About five minutes, and the poison should kick in. You'll be knocked onto your ass."

"If I do, you better not try anything while I'm dead."

A chuckle escapes me, and I shake my head at this chick. She's probably the most entertainment I've had in years. It's almost a shame this is business and not pleasure. "Scout's honor."

"Were you actually a Boy Scout, because I think you've pulled that scouts honor shit before."

"No, I wasn't a scout. So, this Harvey, tell me why he rubs you the wrong way."

"I never said he rubbed me. Never. The thought of that is just … disgusting."

As amusing as this is, it's going to take hours to keep this girl focused.

"But if you must know, I'm apparently his Tom Hardy."

"You're what?"

"His free pass. His fuck fantasy. Whatever sick thing swingers call it."

Now we're getting somewhere.

"He left me a note. Telling me he wanted to strangle me, or rape me. I get to choose. Isn't that sweet? I get a choice." She chuckles again on another hiccup.

Meanwhile, her words hit my blood like a frost, turning everything cold and numb. *Carl.* Perhaps it's the taunting nature of the note—providing two horrible outcomes—that reminds me so much of my childhood, when Carl would have me choose between two evils. A manipulative means of lessening his own guilt, by making me an accomplice to my own nightmare.

Kill the cat, or skin the fur off its tail. You pick. His words chime in my memory, and I've no doubt the note Nola received wasn't from Harvey. A cunning killer has chosen her, and she thinks it's some swinging cock looking for a gang bang. There *is* a connection to Harvey, one I haven't yet made in my head, but for now, I have a vehicle to track, one that has ties to Nola, and that's better than nothing.

"He signed it *Sweet Dreams.*"

A play on his moniker.

Jesus Christ.

She doesn't even realize the shit storm she's been swept up in. Bad karma doesn't even begin to describe the situation.

"When was this?"

"Other night. When I left work."

"Did you report it to the police?"

"My brother's a cop. I could've. I should've. Jonah would probably sever Harvey's nuts, though, and then he'd get in trouble for that. He doesn't need all that right now. 'Sgotta lot going on."

Of course her brother's a cop. And I'll be sure to take my time wringing Jackson's neck for his scrupulous research skills.

"This Harvey sounds like a piece of work." I have no intentions of encouraging her to go to the police about the note. Better to go along with her story.

"Wan' know how I got m'name, Voss? My parents had sex. In Nawlins." Snorting a laugh, she rubs her hand over her face and bites her bottom lip. "They got it on drunk. So it's only fitting I'm drunk, right? I'm an oops baby." She sighs, resting her chin against her palm that slips from beneath her. "I think … I don't know what's wrong with me. I think I'm getting … tired. Need to close … my eyes."

With a hearty yawn, she rests her head against her palm once more, and eyes closed, she asks, "What'd you say again?"

I don't answer, and instead tip my head, watching her chest move up and down, her mouth gape while she slowly succumbs to sleep. When her head plops onto her outstretched arm, passed out, I push up from the table and take the last sip of my wine, before setting the glass back down.

I pull her chair back, and as her head wobbles like a rock on a toothpick, I scoop her up into my arms.

"Mmm y'smellrealgoo." She mumbles incoherently, wrapping her arms around my neck, as I carry her up the stairs. Oddly enough, I like the way she feels against me, tucked into my chest.

I pass two closed doors until I find a large spacious bedroom at the end of the hall. The lace and heavy wood furniture reminds me of my mom's room when I was a kid, a little outdated, but feminine and warm.

Laying her down on the bed, I take in the scent of her—a sweet vanilla and peaches that hits my jaw with the urge to bite down into that creamy flesh. Standing over her, I run my hand down over her jaw, to her throat, and grind my teeth at the thought of squeezing her there, then down to her collarbone, over her shoulder toward her breast. The intense desire to grope her is stamped out by the visual of her tied up and blindfolded, passed out, just as she is now, while I fuck her unresisting body. So unnatural.

Clamping my eyes closed, I step away from her. From those thoughts.

To fulfill that fantasy, she'd have to be a willing participant. That's the rule that's kept my control in check. The one thing that ensures I'll never be like my uncle, or my grandfather.

My brand of sex would terrify an innocent thing like Nola, though, whose diet is probably strictly vanilla. She'd never submit to something so depraved, so as far as I can see, she's nothing but a lovely piece of art to admire from afar. An unwitting little canary who's captured the attention of a starving wolf.

Brushing my knuckles across her cheek, I move a strand of hair from her eyes and stare down at her peacefully sleeping face.

Not exactly hard to watch her closely. With my focus still on her, I back myself out of her room, and close the door behind me.

Hot steam seeps over the top of the shower as I undress. In the mirror's fogged reflection, the scar across my eye sticks out from my face like an ominous reminder of why women like Nola are off the menu for me. I'll never have something so normal, so unsullied. The night I was given this scar changed everything. It turned a decent kid into a criminal, and eventually, a man into a monster.

The craving inside of me is a black hole, a void that'll never be filled. As if my insides have been hollowed over time, leaving me starving for something darker, more sinister, with every climax. I can't deny that a fucked-up childhood played a major role in my violent nature. The intersection between a sordid past and my pleasure is a consummation unfulfilled, a temptation I won't indulge in, for fear that I would be just like the men who raised me.

Men who found sadistic joy in harming women.

I'd sooner starve than feed such violent acts, but I can't deny the lure of those sounds and the rush of excitement. The fantasies of having a woman like Nola, strong and defiant, giving me some measure of chase. Taunting whatever primitive part of my brain craves the challenge of conquering something wild and untamable.

I press play on the video. It's staged porn, ridiculous to watch, as the dude reminds me of some old time villain, detailing his nefarious intent in the beginning. Thankfully, he's quiet the rest of the video, and it's only her sounds after. Her muffled cries. Her pleas. Her suffering. Again, all staged, but as real as it gets for me.

Once inside the shower, I let the punishing torrent of water beat against my muscles, and rest my head against the cool tiles as it hammers away the tension. My stomach flexes with the sudden rush of blood that reminds me how much I've come to enjoy my showers. Historically, it's where I've let a number of subs suck me off after work, before indulging in some of our more illicit pastimes. Tonight, it's the sounds of a stranger and the visuals of Nola.

I stroke my hand up and down my shaft, taking a moment to squeeze at each exchange. The scene inside my head opens to Nola, chained to the wall in my dungeon, wearing that tight little waitress uniform hiked to mid-thigh. No panties, or bra, beneath.

She struggles to get free, while the woman's grunts in the video add some dimension to this wicked fantasy. As I approach, the clanging of the chains grows louder, the panic in her voice more audible.

She knows what I want.

Releasing my cock, I take a moment to revel in the torment of wrangling her against me, the need to be inside of her more than I can bear. As she squirms in my arms, her bare ass beneath the skirt brushes across my tip, and my stomach tightens at how soft, how warm she feels.

"Please," the woman's voice echoes in the bathroom. "You don't want to do this."

But I do.

Fist tight around the base of my dick, I imagine pushing inside of her, feeling her body stiffen against mine, her soft cries dying to long-drawn moans. My hips drive forward, and with the heat of the water, I picture burying my dick inside her tight cunt, the chains over her head lifting her tits through the unbuttoned opening of her shirt, enough for me to suck one of her pert pink nipples into my mouth.

She tries to fight it, of course, for the sake of her pride, but the moment her head tips back and those pretty lips part, the moment she relents and owns her pleasure, is the moment my whole body shudders with victory. I pump my cock in time to each thrust, fucking her rough and recklessly, as the chains rattle and her tits bounce in my face. I drive my hips into my palm the same way I drive into her pussy. Hoisting her up, I pin her to the wall, bracing my hand against the cold tiles as the visual plays in tandem with the woman in the video, the sounds of slapping flesh and her outcries.

Tension winds inside my muscles, and I don't take my eyes off Nola because I need to watch her come, even if it's just in fantasy.

The woman's moans heighten. The slapping sounds hasten in time to the wet jerking of my cock.

"Oh, no, please," the woman in the video mewls to her fake captor. "I can't." The beauty of it is how real she sounds, though. The distress in her voice bleeds through every sweet little imploration, until her moans become quick pants and hiccups of panic.

She can't help the inevitable collapse of her resistance, as every muscle trembles with the need to hold on to her tightly-guarded morals, and the moment her pussy contracts along my shaft, I'm done. Warm jets of cum hit the tiles, quickly washed away by the dribbles of water spilling from my skin. I groan and squeeze every drop, imagining my seed up inside of her, filling her body. How badly I wish I could touch her right now, to see the flush of her skin and watch her body convulse in pleasure. Harsh breaths beat back against my face as I rest my head against the shower wall and bang out the last of my load.

It's not enough. It never is.

For now, though, it keeps the cravings under control.

For now, it keeps Nola safe from my messed-up appetite, a bastard family curse that ensures I'll never have a woman the same way most men do.

13

THE SANDMAN

ne week ago …
    The blonde twitched with the first signs the tranquilizer had begun to wear off. The slight flare of her nostrils through the small breathing holes of the latex mask told him she could smell the gasoline in the bucket beside her. The only visible part of her face was her lips, which parted on a gasp. Her eyes remained concealed by black latex that also masked her long blonde hair and covered her body.

Aside from her thick, pouty lips, she no longer had any distinguishable features. She could be anyone he wanted her to be. A faceless doll, like the mannequins he'd once slept with at night. Only, the doll before him was warm and came with a hole in which he could bury his swelling manhood, many times throughout the night.

Long, slender legs jerked beneath the smooth black latex sheet vacuum-sealed to her body, where she lay trapped on a bed, knees bent, her thighs held frog-legged apart by the form-fitting plastic. Her hands had been placed flat to the bed at either side of her, completely immobile.

Every curve visible, teasing him.

The sheets came in a variety of colors—white, clear, red. Black was his favorite, though, and the hole for the head fit snug at the throat, to keep the air locked inside, so he could play with different masks. Some covering the mouth, some the entire face. In this case, he enjoyed the element of fear in having her eyes shielded.

He wore a full body latex suit, himself, but unlike the mask she wore, his offered cutouts not only for the mouth, but the eyes, too. Even his penis fit into a black latex sheath attached to the suit, which he'd buffed with lube—the mere preparation making him fully erect. He couldn't stand the thought of touching her dirty skin, riddled with hair and dry bits that flecked off. The visual of fluids seeping out of her cunt made him want to gag.

The leather braids of his whip slipped between his fingers as he toyed with it, waiting for her to wake.

With a drowsy groan, she shook inside the sheet of latex in a poor effort to move about.

The first weak scream that passed her lips soured to a tearless sob. Latex squeaked and rubbed as she fought inside her bindings.

"Hello, Marnee."

At the sound of his voice, she froze, lips trembling as her head, the only movable part of her body, blindly shifted back and forth, as though she searched the air for him.

Dipping his latex-clad finger into the gasoline, he dabbed a small drop beneath her nose, and she reared back, gasping through her mouth. "Regarding my proposition earlier …" He reached down to where the base of a red dildo stuck out of an attached condom he'd jammed into her pussy—a long latex balloon pocket he'd sewn into the sheet to keep the air from leaking out. With a gentle tug, he removed the plug for the small hole between her pried thighs, one he could scarcely look at, even when covered in the shiny black material, without shivering. "Which would you prefer? To be ravaged for hours, or burned alive?"

"Please." Her voice carried a slur, broken by sniffles. "Don't do this. Please don't do this."

"Answer the question."

"I want to go home."

Whip in hand, he brought the leather braids down against her thighs with a resounding whack that echoed through the cold pole barn.

She cried out, while the latex concealed the marks of her abuse.

Bent forward, he ran his hands over the smooth black sheet and kissed her. Oh, the remorse on her lips. They all felt remorse at that point.

Her face scrunched with another sob. "Please ... just let me go. I can't ... I can't feel my arms. Or my legs."

"No, you can't. And you won't. You'll be paralyzed, either burning alive, or letting me fuck you. Your choice."

"Why? Why can't I—"

He silenced her question with a sharp slap to her face, kicking her head to the side. "Tell me which you'd prefer. The longer you procrastinate, the worse it will be for you. Can you even imagine how it would feel, having your skin burn inside latex without being able to move a muscle? How terrifying that would be, as it sticks to your skin."

"I'm sorry." Her body convulsed with a sob. "If I ... did something. If I hurt you, somehow." They all played that game—trying to appeal to some empathy that just didn't exist.

"You're really not. But that's okay. Tonight, you will be made virtuous again. Now, tell me what you want. Fire? Or me?"

Only the whimpers and the downward curve of her lips served as evidence of her crying.

"I understand. I'll grab a match."

"No! Wait! I choose you!"

"Really? You're not just telling me that? You'd really rather have me?"

"Yes."

"I knew ... I knew you were special." He trailed a finger over her latex-covered face, catching the subtle flinch of her muscles. "Oh, Marnee, when I'm finished with you, your soul will be cleansed, and the world will be right again."

"You'll let me go?"

"No, are you saying you want to go? Were you *lying* moments before?"

"No, I wasn't lying. I promise."

"Good." Cupping her cheek, he planted another kiss to her lips, taking in the feel of her latex against his. He'd lubed the mask beforehand to keep it from squealing during contact, as the sound often distracted him.

Round pert breasts stuck out through the plastic, so skintight to her body he could grab her hard nipple through it. He took a moment to grope them, studying her face for any sign of disgust. "Don't be ashamed. It's not your fault you're turned on right now."

The sheet shook with her sob, as he fondled her. The bed's steel frame had been bolted to the floor, so as not to shift around with even the most vigorous movement.

"Do you like how that feels, Marnee?" One of the things he most enjoyed about the latex, particularly against his cock, was that it enhanced the sensation of touch. With the added lube and scent of rubber on the air, he could hardly contain the pre-cum warming the inside of his sheath.

A whine escaped the woman, the only reaction she could

muster with her body still paralyzed, but she nodded. "It ... feels nice."

The shaky quality of her voice betrayed her, but it didn't matter. He wasn't interested in making her feel good. Touching her was his own delight, not hers. She was one of the chosen, and she should feel grateful for what he intended to do.

"Well, since you've been so *honest* with me, it's only right that I'm honest with you. Not everything I do to you is going to feel nice. In fact, you may experience excruciating pain at some point. But nothing like being burned alive. I promise."

She broke into sobbing again, and he stroked her shiny, black skull.

"Shhhh. You made the right choice, Marnee. Tonight, you will accept my seed. I will fill your body with it, and you will be mine. My beautiful possession." Of course, none of his ejaculate would truly end up *inside* of her, as it would remain trapped inside the sheath, but the act itself represented his possession of her.

He pushed to his feet and made his way to the foot of the bed. Legs spread apart, her clitoris sat somewhere beneath the sheet, and thankfully, he couldn't see it. Nausea churned in his gut at the thought of his dick rubbing against the ugly, discolored flesh. The idea of such a thing sickened him, and he looked away as he pushed his hips forward. In a blind attempt to find her hole, he jabbed his tip into her, cringing at the realization he'd hit her clit.

Warm walls sucked him inside, the balloon like a hot glove gripping tight to his cock.

Lying perfectly still, she cried out, while he rocked into her, and with a few easy thrusts, his mind was lost to the softness and the overpowering scent of latex that put him at ease.

"You can't fight me, anymore. You can no longer reject

me, Marnee. I can do whatever I want to you. And I promise you, I will."

———

Hours passed. He'd already had his way with her twice, her body still frozen in the latex, accepting his swollen cock as she milked his precious nectar.

As he entered to have his way with her again, he pushed against her throat, squeezing it. She gasped and moaned, while his body heightened toward climax, and when he orgasmed a third time, she didn't make a sound.

Curious, he released her, head tipped as he studied her for any movement.

Blue gaping lips and her motionless chest confirmed he'd strangled her to death already. As connected as he could possibly be. The ultimate possession of another human being. Almost God-like.

He bent forward to listen for breath and heard nothing. Still, he didn't pull out of her. He quite liked staying there a bit longer, and settled down on top of her body, resting his head on her cold, stiff breasts.

So beautiful.

———

Fine grains of sand slipped through his hand as he stared down at her empty sockets, from where blue eyes once stared back at him.

He hadn't meant to kill her so quickly. He'd merely gotten caught up in the moment, excited at watching her struggle to breathe while he fucked her. But he'd hoped to keep her until dawn, and two hours remained until then.

The ruffling of leaves whispered around him as he poured

the sand into her eyes, while she lay on a bed of frost-coated foliage he'd piled beneath her. The sand made it easier to look at her, made her less terrifying.

From the ground beside her, he picked up a half-bloomed Queen of the Night he'd clipped from his green-house and set it carefully in her crossed arms. Always the same way, because consistency was everything.

He'd scrubbed her vagina clean, douching her insides with oxidizing bleach so as to destroy any evidence he may have left there. Afterward, he dipped her whole body in a tub of pure bleach and a small bit of lye he often used when tanning animal hides.

With the FBI's involvement, he couldn't be too careful.

Staring down at her pale, dead face, he felt the compulsion to kiss her, to stroke an ungloved finger down her now-clean face, but he knew better. She'd be scoured for evidence, and the small clues he'd already made a point to place were to be the focus of her murder investigation. He didn't need any small trace fibers getting in the way of his signatures.

Besides, he could rest easy, knowing she would always be his. From that night on, and forever, her body, her entire being, belonged to him alone.

She was pure. Clean. No longer tainted by her paltry principals that made her a snobby bitch.

No. She'd become virtuous and delicate as porcelain. No one else would ever lay claim to her. Every piece of her belonged to him.

He lifted the pickle jar filled with formaldehyde solution and Marnee's beautiful blue eyes. His only wish was that he could always remember how breathtaking they looked with her tears.

His little flower had blossomed that night. Had chosen him over everything else, and had taken him with her into eternal sleep. A piece of him would forever live within her.

14

NOLA

A loud incessant sound cracks through the void, jarring me out of dreams. As my eyes flip open to the surrounding darkness, I snap my head toward the alarm clock, and army crawl toward it. After slamming my hand against the snooze button, I bury my face in the pillows.

Bits of my dream still linger, keeping me in a semi-lucid state as I turn my head to the side, the events from the night before creeping into my slowly-dawning consciousness.

The last thing I remember is telling Voss about my job. And Harv.

And that my parents conceived me in New Orleans.

Burying my face again, I groan. Why the hell would I tell him that?

I perform a quick pat down, mentally noting my pants and shirt still in place.

So, did I stumble to bed and pass out, or pass out first? Did Voss put me to bed?

Lifting my head, I slam my face into the pillow over and over, stirring the beginnings of a headache. Guy could've done a million and one things to me in my sleep, but there's no evidence to suggest he did any more than help a tipsy idiot not fall down the stairs to her death.

Christ.

Of course, I have a deeply-rooted desire to believe Voss is a decent person, because if there's one thing I can't stand, it's being wrong about someone. Even so, I'll never be able to face this guy again, and if he doesn't already think I'm a freak, well, that's a problem in itself.

It comes as a surprise that my head isn't throbbing like yesterday, when I swore there were rhinos bouncing on pogo-sticks inside my skull. "Must've been good wine," I mutter, stumbling out of the bed toward the bathroom.

I brush my teeth and relieve myself quickly, before nabbing my phone off the nightstand on my way out of the bedroom.

Oliver's bedroom door is cracked, and I peek inside to find him sleeping. Moving to beside his bed, I'm taken back to the days when he was just a baby, asleep in his crib, and I could watch him for hours, dreaming of so many things for him in life.

I curse the world for being so cruel to him at such a young age, for proving how shitty some human beings can be. So many days, I wish I could go back to those moments, when he fit in my arms, and I could keep him safe just by holding him.

The moment his form blurs, I quickly shuffle out of his room. I can't get caught up in those thoughts. Not today.

Hustling to downstairs, I enter the kitchen and find an entire pot of coffee already made. Either Voss programmed it, or I was walking around in a drunken, zombie state while performing all my usual bedtime routines.

I make Oliver a quick lunch, then drink a cup of coffee while reading the news on my CNN app. Locally, another girl has gone missing—a young blonde socialite last seen by friends in The Loop. Authorities suspect it's the same guy who swiped up a couple girls before her, whose bodies were found without eyeballs.

Ugh. This is exactly why I hate watching, or reading, the news. Stories like these play on my paranoia, and suddenly every man I know is a suspect.

I click out of the app, then head up the stairs to wake Oliver. My phone buzzes in my back pocket on the way, and I slip it out to see Jonah calling.

"Hey," I say on answering.

"Hey, Diane wanted me to let you know she's going to be about fifteen minutes late grabbing Oli after school. Is he okay to be home for a few?"

"Yeah, he'll be fine." Most likely, he'll come home, sit in his room, and either read, or draw, or blast his music. Either way, he'll keep himself occupied. As a single mom, I've had to make quick runs to the grocery store, leaving him home for a few minutes at a time.

"Okay, cool. How's the new roommate working out?"

"Voss? He's … not bad. Keeps to himself mostly, but not in a creepy way."

"Good. You'll tell me if anything goes awry."

"Duh. And thanks for giving me a heads-up for today. I'll let Oli know to wait on the front porch for her."

"All right. Talk later. Love you."

"Love you more," I say, before hanging up the phone.

One thing I always regretted was never giving Oli a sibling. Just wasn't in the cards with Denny. We tried when Oliver was two, but a half dozen miscarriages later, and I was tired. Tired of crying, tired of hoping, but mostly, tired of feeling like a broken woman. I think a sibling might've changed things, though. There were times when I couldn't talk to my mother, but things just came easy with Jonah. Not even Nora and I had the kind of bond I shared with my brother.

"Hey," I say softly. "Time to wake up, Oli."

As usual, he doesn't say a word, but huffs and rolls over in bed.

"C'mon, Champ. I know you're tired, but you have to get up."

Seconds pass, and he doesn't move.

"Oliver, you have to get up, baby. It's time for school."

Still no movement.

I pad across his room to beside his bed and give a light shake of his arm. "Hey, I hate having to get up for work, but that's the breaks, kid."

He shoves my hand away, burying his face in the pillow.

"What's going on?"

When he turns to face me, I catch the shine of tears in his eyes.

Worry blooms in my chest. "Oli? What's wrong, baby?"

His brows come together as he lets out a quiet whimper, and for a moment, I think he's going to open his mouth and speak for the first time in months. Instead, he breaks into a quiet sob.

"Oliver? Did something happen last night?" My first thought is that I let a man, a stranger, into my house, and passed out drunk while my son was left alone with him. The kind of thing only a truly shitty mom would do.

A thought that stirs nausea in my gut, as I watch him curl into himself, until he shakes his head, setting my guts free of the anxiety. I'll punish myself later for my irresponsibility, but for now, my focus is finding out what makes my son, who hasn't cried in months, suddenly break into sobbing.

"Voss didn't come into your room, or anything?"

He shakes his head, wiping away the tears.

"Are you sad? Did you have a bad dream about your dad again?"

Again, he shakes his head.

"God, I wish you'd tell me, baby. I'd give anything to hear you tell me what's wrong." I stroke his hair and thumb a tear from his cheek. "Did something happen at school?"

He doesn't answer at first, and a million days seem to slip through my head all at once, on a desperate search to remember an instance when he might've tried to tell me something before, and I was just too preoccupied with my own shit.

But he shakes his head.

"Do you want to write it down?"

He lets out an exasperated breath and pushes my hand away, while he sits up in bed. Just like that, his emotions are sucked away into an invisible vacuum, leaving me with more questions than answers. If I cracked this kid open, he'd probably have unaddressed anger and resentment spilling out of him like a piñata.

"Oliver … I may not be the wisest person in the world, but you're the most important person in mine. If something's bothering you, or if something happened, you'll tell me, yeah?"

Tucking his knees close to his body, he nods.

"Okay. Whenever you're ready, just … come to me. I'm all ears, okay?"

He nods again.

"Okay. I'll see you downstairs." I pat his leg and push up from his bed, before making my way downstairs. Every day, I feel like I'm losing the little boy who wanted nothing more than to cuddle with me when I first woke him up in the morning. As he grows older, I feel as if his heart is becoming harder, more impenetrable. That his anger has begun to outweigh his love.

After a quick breakfast, I shuffle Oliver off to school and hop in the shower. Ten minutes later, I'm out the door, wet hair and all.

On Mondays, I work afternoons, which gives me time to do some much-needed grocery shopping. Poor Oli had both heels of bread for his peanut butter sandwich this morning.

I actually hate buying food, and look forward to the day I can push a button and it all arrives in some huge pneumatic tube, conveniently organized in my refrigerator. But until then, I wheel the Explorer into an open spot at the end of the row of the grocery store lot, feeling like every other normal person who drives a fully functioning vehicle, for once in my life. No worrying about whether, or not, the damn thing will start when I leave the store.

With the extra money from Jonah and Diane, coupled with what Voss gave me, I feel like a woman who can buy the expensive granola and body wash. And another delight? Not having to worry whether, or not, the transaction will go through.

In a matter of thirty minutes, my cart is full of things that, just a week ago, I couldn't afford, and I head to check out.

"How are you feeling, *Star Wars*?" The deep velvet voice tickles my ear, as I wait to unload my cart, and I turn to find Voss in line behind me.

Tall and intimidating, he looks damn near edible in his black button-down shirt and jeans. There's something about this man I can't quite put my finger on. Something wild and terrifying beneath that tightly-composed mask he wears, like a thunderstorm trapped behind the thin veil of a cloud. I have a feeling if ever he decided to cut loose, he'd wreak havoc on whatever crossed his path.

His basket holds a bottle of liquor, wine, some vegetables, cat kibble, which means he *hasn't* gotten rid of the kitten yet, and a few granola bars. Not unusual to find him here, seeing as it's the closest store to where we live, just strange seeing him out in public. Like running into a wolf while out in the woods.

Heat rushes over me in waves as the memories from the night before remind me I have much to be embarrassed about in this encounter.

"Not bad. Not good," I tell him. "Am I to assume it was you who put me to bed?"

"Were you expecting someone else helped you?"

"I'm … sorry for that. I don't drink often, but when I do, it's a disaster. I don't typically talk … so *freely*."

"I'll keep that in mind."

"So, we're on the same shopping schedule?"

"I'm just here to pick up a few things."

"The essentials, I see."

"I like my whiskey … almost as much as watching you polish off a bottle of wine by yourself." The amusement in his voice is an annoyance that I find oddly attractive. A hate to like sort of thing that has me both irritated from the embarrassment and strangely drawn to his cockiness.

"Well, I hope you took a picture, because that isn't happening again."

"Said the girl who nursed a hangover the day before that."

"You really enjoy getting on my nerves, don't you?"

"I enjoy getting on lots of things, but your nerves has quickly become my favorite."

"I'll keep that in mind."

I pay for the groceries, and Voss walks me out to my car —uninvited of course, but I appreciate the gesture, particularly when he loads the bags into the trunk.

"For a Wall Street Wolf, you're awfully polite."

"Perhaps you've found my inner sheep."

I chuckle at that, standing just outside the propped driver door.

In a few steps, he invades my personal space, crowding me against the car in a way that trips my body harm alarms. He leans forward, and I swear I can hear my pulse in my own ear when his warm breath fans my neck. The crinkle of a bag draws my attention to the bottle shaped sack he sets on my driver seat behind me. The bottle of wine, I'm guessing. "We'll keep that our secret, yeah?"

My blood is burning, hands trembling at my side. Not only does he smell incredible, but he gives off a sort of electricity that stuns in such close proximity. When I nod, he leans into me again, keeping his lips close to my throat.

I close my eyes to the visuals of him kissing me right here in the middle of the parking lot.

"You have a nice day, Nola." The deep timber of his voice oozes raw masculinity, and the temperature of my body becomes apparent the moment he steps away from me and a coldness filters in between us.

I open my eyes to see him heading toward his car with the kind of cocky stride that only some men can pull off. The kind belonging to a powerful man who truly doesn't give a shit what you think of him.

A glance down at my hands shows white knuckles gripping the window frame—a clear sign that the man sends my body into a state of defense.

I slip my apron over my head and hop along the serving counter as I tug my shoes on. "Hey, Dale, where's Bethany?"

"No call. No show." Disappointment clings to his voice as he glances around at the diner that's packed on a Monday afternoon. "Josie's coming in at two, but this place is getting nuts. If you'd been one minute later, I'd been chewin' your ass."

"Your teeth will never come close to my ass, Dale." I try to lighten the mood, but I feel his stress. It's going to be a busy one today.

"Your buddy in the corner refuses to be served by anyone else." With an irritated grumble, he gives a slight jerk of his head. "Might want to start with him first. He's been here for about twenty minutes, waiting for you."

Twisting around, I find Simon sitting in the corner booth with a half-drawn smile, and he waves to me. Earlier than his usual time.

"Oh, boy," I mutter, mostly to myself. This should be interesting. Rejection has never really been my thing, and I didn't want to put him in the position of being slapped with it, but he asked me, and I don't do dates.

When I spin back around, something on Dale's collar draws my attention. A red splotch against the white fabric. "What happened there? You got … something red. Is it ketchup?"

In an instant, he slaps his hand against his neck, cheeks flushed, as he steps away from the serving counter. "I cut myself shaving this morning. That's gross."

His face pinches to disgust, as if a little bit of blood is a big deal.

"Dale, I had a husband. Who shaved. And cut himself, sometimes. I don't consider that to be all that gross. Maybe try vinegar to get it out of the fabric."

"Thanks," he says, making his way toward the sink across the kitchen.

I finally head over to Simon, trying to muster a friendly, non-awkward smile. "Hey, Simon, what can I get ya?"

"I just want to start out by saying I'm sorry. For asking you out."

"You don't have to apologize for that."

"You lost your husband. It was … too soon. I admire that in you."

That's not the only reason, but I nod, anyway. "It's been rough for Oli and me."

"I don't … do that often. I just want you to know."

"I understand. You took a chance. Nothing wrong with that."

"It is, though. It's wrong to take advantage of a grieving woman."

"Really, Simon. You're beating yourself up over nothing." At the flinch of his brows, I clear my throat. "I don't mean nothing. I just mean, I don't think bad of you for asking. So, how 'bout we start over. What can I get ya?"

"Usual. Grilled cheese. No crust. Fries. Ketchup on the side, and a glass of milk."

"Got it." I jot his order down and stuff the pad and pen into my apron. "You haven't heard from Beth, or Harv, have you?"

Lips pursed, he shakes his head. "My guess? Those two probably hooked up with the wrong person."

Perhaps it's a disturbed look on my face that has Simon's eyes widening, and he lurches in the booth. "Oh, I didn't mean that. It was … a joke."

I can't lie. I've sometimes wondered the same thing, as often as they take in strangers, but hearing someone else say it aloud is like giving life to a forbidden thought.

I'm more inclined to believe the two of them packed up and skipped town, but Beth is such a braggart, I can't imagine her not telling anyone. I can't imagine her skipping work, either, as often as they bitch about money.

"Let's hope you're wrong."

15

VOSS

Parked across from Duli's Diner, I have the perfect view of Nola's rental vehicle parked off to the side. And after an hour of watching it, I've come to the realization that I'd never make it as a full-on stalker. Staking someone out has to be the most boring fucking job in the world. In this case, Nola makes it worth the suffering, as good as she looks in her little waitress uniform, but as a general rule, sitting idle is enough to make me want to stab my eyeballs out with a toothpick. I don't mind hunting someone down, it's the long hours of watching, waiting to catch a glimpse of prey, that whittles at my patience. I'm convinced, wherever she is, though, I'll find my quarry.

It's been an hour, and I've witnessed about two dozen people come and go. The white van is nowhere in sight, and neither is anyone who looks remotely like Carl.

Not that I'd necessarily recognize him nowadays. It's been nearly twenty years since the night I took off. My mind swirls with memories of his face in what few details come to mind, but all I can see is a vague image, a mask of indifference. The face of a kid who'd been bred not to care about anyone, or anything.

"*Boo!*" *Carl leaps out in front of me on my way to my bedroom.*

I fall back against the wall behind me, eyes locked on what looks to be an expressionless mask, though it's hardly discernible in the surrounding darkness of the corridor. "*What the hell is that?*"

He snickers, tipping his head to the side. "*What's the matter? Scared?*"

Not wanting to admit every bone in my body is shaking, I frown and push off the wall. "*No. But what's it for?*"

"*If I told you, I'd have to kill you.*"

Through the holes in the mask that's made from papier-mâché, I'd guess, I can see his eyes, focused on me. "*Better make sure grandfather doesn't see you. He'll be pissed you used all his newspaper for that.*"

"*What makes you think it's newspaper?*"

"*What else would it be?*"

"*Feel it. Unless you're too chicken.*"

I reach up to touch the mask, but hesitate, drawing my hand back. "*Just tell me.*"

"*See if you can guess.*" *Always a game with Carl.*

My fingertips make contact with the smooth surface, and at the soft, almost rubbery texture, I wrench my hand back. "*What did you do?*"

"*Relax. It's not human.*"

"*What is it, then?*"

"*Remember the cat I skinned?*"

Horror prickles my nerves at the memory of hearing the cat screaming. "*How ... did you ... with the fur?*"

"*Soaked it. Used grandfather's flesh knife.*"

I gulp back the urge to throw up at the thought that he's

wearing a cat's skin on his face. One he tortured and mutilated in fun. "You're sick."

"You know what's sick? Dirty little whores who think it's funny to play games. Let's see how they like my game."

"What are you talking about, Carl?"

"We'll see how funny it is when they're scared shitless. When they scream. Just like that cat."

I stare through the windshield, still lost to memories. Wasn't until I got to high school that I learned some of the cruel shit the other kids did to him. Legendary stories passed down by the upperclassmen about how they *tamed the freak*, by giving him swirlies in the girls' bathroom, how they snuck a used tampon into his sandwich, or let him touch a few of the cheerleaders tits, only to turn around and have the football players beat his ass for fondling them.

I did my best to hide the fact that we were blood, but when word got out, I faced my own version of hell, both in and out of school. Wasn't a girl in the state of Illinois who'd date the freak's nephew. I'd have probably been just as isolated and cold, if not for my mother and the hope she instilled in me to break free, someday.

The masks he wore eventually evolved into a variety of skins—innocent animals he captured and tortured in fun. Their carcasses littered the woods of the estate, the empty eye sockets filled with ground bone, so fine, it almost looked like sand. I never understood why he bothered with such a ritual, but my guess is, even he couldn't stand to see the emptiness staring back at him. Other critters eventually ate their remains before my mother, or grandfather, found them, but it wouldn't have really matter if they had. He found a way to earn my grandfather's approval when he learned taxidermy, and would offer gifts he horrifically mutilated and preserved.

He became obsessed with the eyes, which I found pinned

to walls in the back shed where he worked, along with a female mannequin he told my mother and grandfather he used to create art. We all believed him, until I caught him carrying the damn thing into his bedroom one night. After some time, he moved on to his preferred prey. Young women —street workers, mostly. When my mother and grandfather were out of the house, I heard him having sex with the women in the next room.

Except, the women were silent.

Drugged and passed out.

He couldn't get off unless they were unconscious. Said he couldn't stand when they tried to talk to him, or ask a bunch of personal questions. He'd have his way with them throughout the night, then dump them on the side of the road somewhere, without paying them a dime, before morning. For years, he did this, sometimes bringing me along to pick one up, until he effectively perfected it. His unsettling charm never failed to lure them into the car, but only when he got them home did that charm flip to something evil and sinister. And in his effort to taunt me, he'd make a spectacle out of it, with loud moans and thumping of furniture, his way of throwing it in my face, on nights when I tried to talk him out of it.

Wasn't long before he grew tired of the routine. And when the police started snooping around, he realized dumping them alive was too risky, even if, most times, they couldn't remember his face.

I catch sight of Nola through the diner window, buzzing from table to table. Never still. I wish I could say my only purpose for sitting in that car was to catch a sadistic psychopath, but I'd be lying. Something about the woman intrigues me. Her tenacity and dedication to her son reminds me of my own mother, and truth is, she's not exactly hard on the eyes.

I try not to think too much about her curves, but goddamn, the way she looked in those jeans at the grocery store had me imagining them bunched at her ankles like cuffs. She's an enticement I can't afford. A distraction that'll cost me the game, if I'm not careful.

A couple of hours watching cars and people coming and going, and I'm ready to crawl out of my skin having to sit so long. I'm more likely to stumble upon something significant after her shift, so I fire up the vehicle and head back to the apartment to grab some lunch. Along the way, I catch sight of Oliver, caught up in a circle of three other kids who look at least two grades older, a few blocks from the house. I slow the car to a crawl, and seconds later, it becomes clear the circle is a trap, and Oliver is the mouse, when one of the kids gives a hard thrust to his chest, knocking him back a step.

Oliver adjusts his glasses, and holds his stance.

Admirable, but even the smallest of the other three looks like he could pummel Oliver into a pancake and eat him.

Everything tells me to keep going. He's not my kid. Not my problem. But the bigger kid swings out, knocking Oliver flat on his ass, and something twists inside of me. Maybe it's whatever miniscule amount of empathy I can muster, having been a mouse myself, when I was a kid. Or maybe something about the older kid just rubs me the wrong fucking way.

Regardless, I pull the car to a stop alongside the curb a few houses down, and stare through the rearview as the boys knock him around.

"Don't do it." I close my eyes to extinguish the scene, but the anger remains in the red haze that greets me behind shuttered lids. "C'mon, kid."

I've got too much invested in Nola right now, and hell if I need my conscience getting in the way.

Fuck. I climb out of the vehicle, lighting up a cigarette to ease the frustration of having to give a shit. With a casual stroll, so as not to alert any of the boys getting their jollies off on knocking Oliver to the ground each time he tries to get up, I approach them like a rhino about to stomp all over an ant hill. The older kid pins Oliver to the ground, rears back a fist, and hammers it into his face.

"Talk, Retard! Or I'll rip your tongue out with my bare hands! Quit fucking pretending!"

Good. He got a hit in. Now I have reason for what I'm about to do. Two of the kids back off, as I approach the unwitting one, who apparently hasn't caught a glimpse of me, yet. Nabbing the back of his jacket, I shove my cigarette between my lips, while I wrench him up off Oliver and pin him to a nearby lamppost.

Eyes wide, he stares back at me, mouth gaping as if to scream, and I grip his throat.

Gently, of course.

"The human tongue isn't as easy to rip out as you might think. Not without a hook, or something to grab hold of the muscle. But the windpipe can be crushed with one tight grip."

Beneath my hand, the boy's throat bobs with a harsh swallow.

"Oliver, you know where this kid lives?" A quick glance back shows Oliver pushing up to a sitting position, chest rapidly rising and falling, and he nods, pointing to one of the houses across the street.

"Good." Turning back to the kid, whose face is screwed up in panic like he's about to piss his pants, I inhale a drag of my smoke and blow it in his face, still pinning him with my other hand. "*I* now know where you live. And if I catch you fucking with him again, I'll string you up to this lamppost here by your tighty-whities for the whole neighborhood to see what a shit-stain you are. Do you understand?" I'm bluffing. Obviously. I wouldn't waste a roll of toilet paper on this little shit, let alone a minute more of my time.

But he nods, anyway.

I drop him, letting him slump to the ground, and as all three kids take off in opposite directions, I reach out a hand for Oliver. His nose is bleeding, and the red plum below his eye socket will undoubtedly be black by the time his mom gets home from work.

Oliver slaps my hand away, clambering to his feet with a pissed-off expression, as if I was the one who made his nose bleed.

"Let me tell you something, Oliver. As a kid who grew up on the streets, the last thing you want to do is bite the hand that just bitch slapped your enemies." I tug at the cuffs of my sleeves and straighten my slacks. "You want a ride home?"

Glancing to the right shows the big kid staring out his front window from the house across the street, and Oliver nods, following after me. As I toss my smoke and fall into the driver's seat, I catch Oliver's eyes wandering over the interior of my car.

"Those kids fuck with you every day?"

Eyes directed toward his hands set in his lap, he nods.

"Here's a quick lesson for dealing with shitheads." Arm resting across the back of the seat, I turn to face him. "First, that kid, if he's smart, he won't retaliate, but if he's stupid enough to try, you're not going to let him rattle you. Bullies love that shit, and you don't need to give him the satisfaction. Second, if anyone gets in your face, you always look 'em dead in the eyes. No turning away, like you did back there." I point two fingers at my own eyes to prove my point. "You hold your bat-shit little stare just like you did to me at dinner. Even if he threatens to stab the bastards out of your head, you don't look away. In your mind, you establish your limit before you snap. And let me tell you kid, when you become good at keeping to that limit, they'll see it on your face. The trick is to make them believe that you're a little crazy. Use that mute mouth to your advantage by watching. Observing. You look for weaknesses." I tip my head to guide his eyes to mine. "Use it against them. Understand?"

Fingers fidgeting in his lap, he nods.

"Good." Twisting back in my seat, I fire up the vehicle and head back toward his house. I have a feeling, if the kid could talk, he'd probably blow me away with the shit inside his head, but physically, he's small and weak, which makes him a target. He'll always be a target, unless he starts using that brain of his to protect what he lacks in strength.

Without doubt, the savvy mind can wreak more havoc than brawn. Carl was a fine example of what happens when a scrawny kid gets pushed too far. When he constantly redefines his limits for the sake of self-preservation. Smart enough to negotiate his way out of just about anything, but abused too many times to really understand—or care, for that matter.

I keep my eyes on the road, making my way down the block. "You watched your father die?"

With a huff, he turns toward the window, then glances back toward his hands before nodding.

"I watched my mom die, too. You and I, we're a different breed, Oliver. We already know the worst kind of pain. The pain of knowing no one can ever really protect you from the bad shit."

With the driveway in view, I glance over at him, where he seems to stare off at nothing. He's a hard read, this kid. Can't tell if a single word I've spoken has made it through his skull, or if I'm just an old man wasting his breath on what will probably be the next school shooter.

"Anyone ever teach you how to incapacitate someone using pressure points?"

Eyes wide, he shakes his head for the first time, telling me he might be absorbing some of this crap, after all.

"C'mon. I'll show you a few tricks I know."

16

VOSS

"With the identification of a new victim found along a popular hiking trail this afternoon, police are urging young women, particularly between the age of twenty-to-thirty years old, to be extremely cautious, especially after dark. Marnee Bucker is the latest victim in a series of murders that have baffled police. The unknown suspect, referred to by the media as The Sandman, is considered both cunning and dangerous. Police are strongly advising that anyone out after dark walk in groups and avoid areas with little to no lighting."

I turn the radio down. Another woman found dead. I saw the news report earlier—Marnee Buckner. Of course, the finer details came from Jackson. Eyeballs missing and filled with sand. Flower in her hands—that one's new. Maybe old age has made him a bit more sentimental about his kills, using the rare breed of flower my mom used to grow in her greenhouse.

Night settles over Belmont Avenue, quiet and serene, like something out of a retro photograph from the fifties. Parked across from Duli's Diner, I watch the place for any sign of the white van I saw before, but the only thing consuming my attention is the brunette through the window, hustling from table to table, busting her ass for those measly tips. Mesmerizing the way the chick fights for a piece of this city like her life depends on it.

I hate stakeouts, but I could watch *her* for hours.

I have watched her for hours.

Sinking into the leather seat, I lean back against the headrest and reach down to adjust the painful hard-on I've worked up from watching those curves work for their perfect shape.

I try not to think about her thighs straddling me right now, or how easily her tits could fit in the palm of each hand, but my body, the torturing bastard, won't relent those visuals. Her moans probably sound breathy and soft, like angel porn, or something.

I rub a hand down my face and blow out an exasperated breath.

That's when my eyes latch onto movement in my periphery. A figure strolling down the empty sidewalk toward the parking lot, hands tucked inside his pants, hood pulled up over his head, concealing his face. I'd blow him off as a hood-rat, if he didn't turn into the diner's parking lot, right up to the only red SUV parked there.

He fiddles around on the windshield, and I open the door of my car, keeping my eyes on him as I tuck my gun into my side holster. Once out the vehicle, I cross the street, picking up the pace, when the stranger walks away from the SUV and back onto the sidewalk ahead of me. I kick it up a notch, to a light jog, and the moment he hastens his pace, it's obvious he knows someone is following behind. Before he can leap into a jog, I nab his collar from behind and drag him into a nearby alley.

Dodging a swing, I slam him against the wall and tear back his hoodie to show a young adolescent face, staring back at me with both fear and confusion.

"Who are you?"

"M-m-my name's Jared."

"What's your business here, Jared?"

"J-just on my way home."

Bullshit. He's lucky I don't interrogate kids the same way I do criminals, because this little bastard has liar written all over his face. "You left something. Back at the car. What was it?"

"I didn't leave anything, man. Like I said, just trying to get home."

I pull my gun, holding it to the kid's shoulder. "You either tell me, or I'll blow your shoulder off."

"Wait, wait, wait. So ... this guy. He paid me fifty bucks to drop off a note on the red SUV parked at Duli's Diner."

"What guy? What'd he look like?"

"I didn't see him. It was dark. He was in a white van."

"When?"

"About ten minutes ago."

Shoving the gun back into its holster, I release him and glance toward the mouth of the alley. "He say anything to you?"

"Just that he needed me to drop the note off. I swear I don't know anything else."

"Get the hell out of here," I say, giving him a light shove.

Out of the alley, I head back toward the parking lot and come to a stop beside Nola's SUV. In addition to the note, there's a picture, and I lift it from beneath the wipers. It's a polaroid of a woman lying on what appears to be leaves, her eyes filled with sand. The lighting seems to be either dawn, or dusk, it's hard to tell, but it gives just enough visibility to see some of the details. Blonde hair and peachy skin that could easily be Marnee Buckner, the woman from the news report. In her hand is a Queen of the Night flower. Not only a tell-tale signature for police, but a sure bet I know the killer.

I glance around, eyes scanning the parking lot, the streets, the adjacent lot, for any sign of the white van, but there's nothing. All is quiet and still.

The accompanying note says "*Mine eternal*" in typed letters across a small scrap of paper.

"Voss?" The familiar voice from behind steels my muscles, and as I turn to face Nola, I shove the note and photograph into my pocket. Eyes narrowed, she tips her head, lifting the strap of her purse up onto her shoulder. "What are you doing here?"

"I think I might've scared someone off. A white van. Pulled up a few minutes ago." A lie, but the knit of her brows tells me she's buying it.

Shaking her head, she glances to the road and back. "Fucking Harv. Bethany didn't come to work today. Two of them must've played hookie. He probably tried leaving me another creepy note. Is that what you stuffed in your pocket?"

"No." Reaching back into my pocket, I tug out the pack of smokes tucked beside the note and photograph, and wave it in front of her. "Was about to have a smoke when you walked up."

"Well, thanks for heading him off." Stuffing her hands into her apron pockets, she looks painfully sexy right now. "Why are you here, though?"

I shove the cigarette between my lips and light it up to buy me some time coming up with an excuse. Thumb scratching across my jaw, I clear my throat. "Another girl's body was found earlier. Didn't think you should be going home late by yourself."

"Yeah." The dubious tone of her voice tells me she doesn't

believe it, and she shouldn't. She shouldn't trust anyone right now, including me. "You drove all the way to my work to see me to my car?"

"Is that strange?"

"Very."

"You don't believe me."

"No. I'd like to think men were that chivalrous, but I know better."

Smart girl. "Then, I'm just going to lay it on you, Nola. I can't stop thinking about you. It's driving me fucking crazy. Crazy enough to drive all the way over here and tell you so." The words are nothing but a cover, but even I'm surprised at how easily they fall from my mouth, like truth.

"Um. Wow. Thank you. For that. Uh … thank you for driving over here."

"What are you doing tonight?" I could kick my own ass for asking that, the shit pouring out of me, like this is some normal encounter between us.

"Pottery," she says, much to my relief. "Lots of pottery. I have a show in a week, and I'm desperately trying to build up my inventory."

"That's too bad. Thought I'd see about making it two for two on the wine."

Her lips stretch to a shy smile. "Ah, definitely not tonight." It's dark, but I swear she's blushing. "But will you take a raincheck? Maybe after my show this weekend?"

"Sure. After your show."

"Good. So, have a good night, Voss."

Instead of answering, I lift her hand and kiss the back of it. "'Night."

After helping her into her car, I watch her drive off, eyes scanning the surroundings one more time. If he's watching me right now, he's aware of one thing: how closely I'm watching her.

Maybe that'll be enough to save Nola from the nightmares.

17

NOLA

Jonah's sitting on the front porch when I pull into my driveway. Strange, as Diane usually drops Oliver off to me on nights I don't drive over myself to pick him up. Typically, the later shifts.

He pushes to his feet, as I make my way toward the front door.

"Everything okay?" I ask.

"Diane picked Oliver up today. He had a black eye."

"What?" I lurch toward the stairs, but Jonah sets his hand on my shoulder.

"He's okay. We iced it, and the swelling's gone down a lot. Diane asked Oliver how he got it. He wrote it down on a piece of paper for her. Claims some kids ganged up on him this afternoon, when he was walking home from his friend's bus stop."

"Dammit! I told him not to get off at Brett's. He knows better than that."

"Well, I'm guessing he knows a lot better now. Anyway, he wrote that Voss scared them off."

"Yeah?" Something about that casts a tingle through my

body, and I have to tamp it down, or risk my brother seeing it written all over my face. "I mean, that's good, right?"

"If he's telling the truth, it sounds like he scared the shit out of the kids."

"You think … Oliver is lying?"

"I think contrary to what you think, he tries to protect you more than you realize."

"What are you suggesting Jonah? That Voss gave him the black eye? Kids are shitheads. Wait 'til you have one." I squeeze my eyes shut and shake my head. "Strike that last comment. I didn't mean anything by it."

"I know you didn't. And no, I'm not calling Oliver a liar. It's my nature to investigate. For both of you."

"Well, I should probably tell you, a few nights back, Harv from my work? He left me a note on my windshield."

Jonah's brows dip, and he unravels his crossed arms like I've just hit the intrigue button. "What kind of note?"

"The lovely kind that asked me if I'd prefer to be raped, or strangled."

"And you're sure it came from Harvey?"

"Pretty sure, yes. He was at the diner the day I found the first note."

By the narrowing of Jonah's eyes, I know I'm in trouble for not saying anything. "Why didn't you tell me this?"

"Because Harv is an asshole. That's relatively mild compared to what he's said to other women, believe me. Anyway, Voss scared him off tonight."

"Voss was at your work?"

"Yeah."

"What for?"

I recall the comment he made about not being able to stop thinking about me. "Nothing I care to go into with you, especially when you're looking at me like that. You don't have to worry about me, Jonah. I'm an adult."

"Yeah, except that another woman was found this morning. A hiker stumbled upon her in the woods."

"I heard that. How'd she die?" While the idea of a woman being found in the woods, dead, is terrifying, with a few women having gone missing lately, *how* has become a common question.

"She had bruises on her neck, and her carbon dioxide levels were high. Coroner thinks she was strangled to death. There were signs of sexual assault, as well. So you need to be careful. Vigilant. Do you have the note Harvey gave you?"

"No. I tossed it."

"Don't toss shit like that. Might be evidence."

"Please don't turn me into another crime scene, Jonah." Harvey Bennington is undoubtedly the biggest prick I've ever met, but he doesn't give me the serial killer, *dump-a-body-in-the-woods* vibe. Particularly if he's stumped someone as smart as my brother, because Harv is a tool. A tool who can barely figure out how to run a washing machine, let alone think to scrub a crime scene for evidence, and I refuse to believe anything else. "I'm trying, desperately trying, not to live my life as a victim every day. I'm trying to give people the benefit of doubt and not view every male I come into contact with as a potential murderer. You know what, though? It's hard. Every day, I'm looking over my shoulder, wondering if the right man is behind bars."

"You think we were wrong. With Denny's murderer."

"No. I want to believe you were absolutely right, because I've had enough bullshit in my life. We both have. It'd be nice to lay something to rest for once."

He stares off, thoughtful, and I don't have to wonder what he's thinking about. Our family is cursed by lack of closure, which has sent Jonah into a tailspin with these missing girl cases. They're too personal for him. "I want to know if this Harvey gets in touch again. If he leaves a note, or tries to contact you, call me immediately."

I nod, but run my fingers through my hair, anxious about one other thing relating to Harvey. "Can you check on Beth? I mean, she didn't come to work today. I'm a little nervous."

"You got an address?"

Rifling through my purse, I tug my phone and text him Dale's number. "My boss should know it. Just tell him I asked you to check on her. He knows my brother is a cop."

Lips pressed to a hard line, he pulls me in for a hug. "Just be careful, okay? This Voss could be anything. Clean record, or not, I wouldn't put too much faith in anyone right now."

"Fair deal. Thanks for dropping Oli off."

"See if you can work some early shifts. This guy targets women at night. Party girls, mostly."

"Well, then, I have nothing to fear. Last I checked they were *rich* party girls, which means, I'm definitely not the killers soup du jour."

"Perhaps not. Doesn't hurt to be careful, though."

"You're right. I'd be foolish to assume anything," I concede.

Offering a pat on my shoulder as he passes, Jonah heads toward his car, and when he drives off, out of view, I glance around one more time at the quiet neighborhood before making my way inside.

Upstairs, I stop at Oliver's room where the door stands cracked, and peek inside. He's already in bed. Considering it's after nine, I'm thankful for that.

I tiptoe across the floor to beside his bed and peel back the blankets covering his face. The streetlamp outside his room offers just enough light to see the black plum around his eye, the sight of which makes me flinch.

Like a slap in the face, I remember this morning, when

Oli woke up for school in tears. He didn't want to tell me what was troubling him, and if I had to guess, he didn't want to go to school.

It makes me wonder if he's been silently dealing with the cruelty of others in the last six months. Here I am, so preoccupied with bringing back the past and trying to restore his innocence that I'm failing to see the present.

Through a blur of tears, I stare down at him, brushing his hair behind his ear. I bend forward and kiss his temple, careful to avoid his eye. "I love you," I whisper, before slinking quietly back through the room.

In the morning, I'll be sure to have a chat with Oliver's school counselor about this, and see about a meeting with this kid's parents, since it happened at the bus stop, but in the meantime, I'm glad Voss was there today.

Wiping my eyes, I pad back down the hall to my bedroom and peer out the window to see Voss's car isn't parked in the driveway, and the lights in the apartment are off. Every instinct inside of me says he's not a bad man, but what if everything I once knew, all the natural inclinations I've spent my entire life paying attention to, have suddenly become mis-wired with Denny's death? What if I no longer recognize the difference between a good and bad man?

Here, I thought Harv was nothing but an annoying asshole with some weird kinks, but what if he's more than that?

What if he's a killer who removes the eyeballs of his victims and stuffs the sockets with sand?

18

VOSS

I glance down at the address Jackson gave me, then back to the shithole bungalow, located on the shady side of town. The white van is nowhere in sight, so I slide out of my vehicle, parked two houses down, and make my way across the street. I should be watching the house where Nola is, but I need to check out Harv and Beth's place first.

Something about this couple just isn't sitting right with me. For whatever reason, Carl has targeted Nola, and although Beth is a more likely target than my landlord, from what I remember of Carl's tastes, I'm guessing she's simply a means to get to Nola. A vehicle he's used to give him a way in.

Whether that's unwitting, or intentional, is still a mystery to me. Carl doesn't take up with accomplices. Even the few times he tried to drag me along on his little escapades when we were kids, he found me to be a nuisance—always getting in his way.

Consequently, I learned to get in his way as much as possible.

From what I've gathered, Beth and Harv are two personalities who would surely bug the shit out of him, so their involvement is likely inadvertent.

Perhaps even deadly, at this point.

The knob on the front door turns easily, and with a gloved hand, I enter the quiet house, gun leading the way. An arc of light cuts through the room when I click on the flashlight and sweep it over the surrounding darkness. Fast food bags and dirty dishes litter the living room, creating a stench of French fries that makes me want to gag. I keep on toward the kitchen, noting the same unkempt condition as the living room, with dishes cluttering the counter, food scattered about. It's a wonder the mice haven't taken over this shithole.

Down the hallway, two rooms stand at either side of the corridor—a bathroom to the left and a bedroom to the right. Entering the one on the right, I take careful steps, so as not to disturb anything, always scanning for movement. Clothes lay about the floor and the bed, but most notable to me are the two pills lying on the mattress, and a glass lying on the floor beside the bed.

Feels hasty and unfinished.

I angle my flashlight up to a chair beside the bed, and when I swing to the right, I see a mirror propped directly across from it.

Must be where Harv sits watching himself jack off, while some dude fucks his wife. I try to imagine my uncle having any part of that, but the idea he'd do anything for the gratification of someone else isn't fitting. He'd only allow someone to watch, if he thought it'd bring them mental anguish. Torment was always his main objective. That's how sadists operate.

The half-opened closet draws my curiosity, and I approach carefully, expecting to find what happened to the couple hanging from the ceiling inside. Instead, I find a collection of BDSM props and gadgets. Some, I recognize from my own arsenal at home—cat-o-nines, paddle, riding crop. I lift a latex suit from where it's crumpled on the floor beside it's packaging, which looks like something sold in a Halloween store, and find an uneven cut along the neck of it.

Weird.

When shadows move across the wall, I flick off the flashlight, dropping the garment to the floor. Slinking along the wall, I duck low and move toward the front of the house, where I peer through the front window.

A car's parked in the driveway. A guy clambers out of the unfamiliar vehicle, a Ford pickup truck, from the looks of it, gun at his hip. I don't recognize him, but then, it's been almost twenty years since I've seen Carl.

Not sure I could point him out from a lineup these days.

As the stranger makes his way toward the front door, I sneak toward the back, looking for a way out. Through the laundry room, there's a backdoor, but it's got so much shit packed against it, there's no way I'd get through without making a bunch of noise. At the first knock, I slip across the hallway back toward the bedroom and attempt to open the window. The window that's been painted shut.

Fuck.

"Hello? Beth? Harv?"

The stranger is inside the house.

As I didn't plan on killing anyone here, I use the butt of my gun to bust out the window.

"Hey!" the stranger shouts from the other room.

I slip through the bashed-out glass, but a streak of pain across my arm leaves me gritting my teeth as I hit the dirt in the backyard. Pushing to my feet, I just make it around the corner, when I see the guy peeking through the busted hole. Hand clamped over my arm, from where blood trails down toward my wrist, I hobble off.

"Stop! Police!"

I don't stop for anything, not even police, and I book it down the street to my vehicle. Once inside, I fire it up and hit the gas, taking off past the house. A quick glance shows the guy dashing out the front door to his truck, but I'm already to the end of the block before I see him hop in the driver's seat through the rearview mirror. After squealing around the corner, I take off up two blocks to the next street and pull into the first empty driveway. I back the car up to the garage and cut the engine, along with the headlights, before ducking down into my seat.

The truck whizzes past me.

With a shaky breath, I exhale and twist my arm, find a nasty gash there that'll undoubtedly need stitches. Hopefully, I didn't leave my fucking DNA all over the glass back there.

Once minutes tick by and the truck seems to be long gone, I drive back out on the street, careful to follow the speed limit, and head back home.

When I arrive, I cut the lights, so as not to draw Nola's attention, and creep up the driveway, slipping past the Explorer, and park in front of the garage. Via the stairs, I enter my apartment, petting Vince on the way to the sink.

From the drawer beside me, I lift a black leather case, one I've learned never to leave home without, filled with first aid items. The sting intensifies when I scrub the wound on the back of my bicep with soap, and I fish through my first-aid bag for a suture kit. Wish I could say this was my first rodeo, sewing up a nasty wound, but it's become something akin to sewing on a goddamn button a few times a year.

I twist the cap off a fifth of whiskey and kick back a nice swill of it, before pouring it over the wound. Teeth grinding inside my skull, I wait for the alcohol to work its magic, then nab a pre-threaded suture. Using the mirror, I try for straight lines with every thread of the needle, but the reflection adds just enough confusion to space them wrong. Thirty minutes later, I'm closing the last stitch, and I snip off the thread and run an alcohol swab over the sutures. A square of gauze fits perfectly over the length of the gash, and I tape it in place.

I've, personally, sewed half the scars on my body. Easier than messing with docs, who ask too many questions.

Bottle in hand, I walk over to the window and kick back another swig, staring down at the breezeway, below where Nola goes to work at her potter's wheel. With the back of my hand, I wipe the excess whiskey from my lips, keeping my eyes locked on her.

Vince brushes past my pants, and I bend down and lift him with one hand, letting him nuzzle himself into my neck. He purrs, when I brush my stubbled face against him and kiss the top of his head.

But my stare remains fixed on the woman.

The longer I spend here, the more I can understand Carl's obsession with her.

With each passing day, I'm finding it harder and harder to look away.

THE SANDMAN

Face hidden behind a latex mask, The Sandman tipped his head, chewing his gum while watching a vacuum suck the air from the bed, on which Harvey lay passed out. Only a small black breathing tube stuck up out of the black latex sheet, one that covered him entirely, without a hole for his head.

At his feet, Beth hung suspended from an upright frame he'd hooked to cables attached to the rafters. Like a latex sculpture, standing vertical, her body completely immobile and vacuum-sealed. Unlike Harvey, though, the latex sheet that covered *her* was blood red and had a hole for the head, the edges of it digging into her neck to maintain the tight seal that held her in place. She wore a mask with holes cut out for the eyes and tiny breathing holes at the nose, her mouth completely covered by the latex.

A different mask to the one Marnee had worn. For a different purpose.

The Sandman got both of them shit-faced drunk, after inviting them to a threesome at his place. His focus was Beth, an obnoxious little bitch he couldn't wait to silence, and Harvey just came as a packaged deal. He didn't like the added body—a risk in terms of breaking his patterns, a breach in keeping the evidence under control—but his torment might prove entertaining.

Rolling her head back and forth, Beth groaned as she slowly came to, and at the first wriggles, he chuckled.

Muffled moans lay trapped inside the covering over her mouth. Her legs squirmed beneath the latex sheet, but failed to get her loose. The moans morphed into little grunts and whispers, as lucidity crept into her voice, and her eyes popped open with panic.

The Sandman stood from his crouch beside Harvey and chomped his gum, studying her fear.

Tears filled her eyes, as she made a muffled plea behind the mask. Always the same routine. Panic. Negotiation. Acceptance. The first few moments were his favorite, though. When realization dawned on their faces and their nightmares came to life. Almost magical.

"Tell me something, Beth. If given the choice, would you choose to let me sodomize you, or watch Harvey suffocate to death?"

Her body shook with a sob, squeaking the latex, the sight of which, made his dick hard. Another imploration failed to break through the covering, but it stoked his anger just the same.

He reached up to slap at her face, watching her eyes blink, and the sounds of panic bled through the plastic. "That's not what I fucking asked you, Beth. Let's try again. Which would you prefer?" Working the gum over his tongue, he blew a bubble in her face, letting it pop.

She startled and fell forward, breathing hard as though hyperventilating in the mask. Even when he grabbed her by the jaw, angling her face back to his, she still gasped for air.

"Quit being dramatic, Beth. Answer the question. Or I'll

have to punish you, and believe me when I say, you will not like my punishment. Now, do you love Harvey?"

With tears streaming down her latex cheeks, she nodded emphatically.

"Do you want to watch him suffocate before your eyes?"

She shook her head back and forth, and made a moaning sound before breaking into another sob.

"Do you choose me, then?"

Gaze falling from his, she nodded and sniffled.

Digging his fingers into her cheeks, The Sandman forced her eyes back to his. "Are you lying to me, Beth? Because I fucking hate liars."

Eyes pleading, she shook her head, and his heart felt light again.

"You truly want *me*."

Another nod nearly had him bursting out of his suit.

"I can't tell you how much this pleases me, Beth. Hang on a second, I want to tell Harvey."

With a skip in his step, The Sandman made his way over to where Harvey lay immobile. He could see the poor bastard's body jerk and spasm beneath the coating of latex that clung to him like a second skin. A vibrating, throaty noise erupted from the breathing tube.

"Listen, Harvey. I just asked Beth who she would choose. And she chose me. I'm sorry, but I guess this means you're shit out of luck." Tugging the wad of gum from his mouth, The Sandman stuck it over the top of the breathing tube, and a sharp scream skated down his spine.

He skipped back to where Beth writhed helplessly in her bindings. "I'm giving you the best of both worlds. But here's the thing. I can't share. I want to fill you with my precious seed, and know that you belong only to me. My little flower of the night. Does that sound okay to you?"

Eyes squinting out more tears, she turned away from him and whined. Whined! Here, he'd offered her the most wonderful gift. To belong to someone far more superior than her nothing husband. And the ungrateful bitch *whined*.

He whopped a hard smack to her face with his knuckles, and her crying lessened to broken sniffles. "You belong only to me. Can you appreciate how special that is? Can you even fathom what a gift it is to be mine?"

Blinking away more tears, she nodded and lifted her gaze to his. Creases beside her eyes offered the smile he couldn't see.

"Don't cry now, Beth. It's time to consummate my possession. To pollinate my little flower, so that when you rest, you'll take a piece of me in dreams. Do you understand? Will you accept me into your body?"

Like with Marnee, he had no intentions of actually touching her dirty cunt, but merely pretending to ejaculate inside of her. After all, neither of the women were actually worthy of his seed.

Her eyes diverted away, tears streaming down the shiny plastic of her face, and she nodded.

With the sounds of Harvey's panic, the muffled screams and the squeal of plastic as he fought for breath, The Sandman pushed a stepping stool behind where she hung, just high enough that his fully erect penis, sheathed in latex, would meet the hole where he'd already inserted a dildo earlier. As he carefully pulled the fully lubed object out of her, so as not to remove the latex condom left up inside her, he heard her gasp. He entered Beth from behind, nervously chuckling as her tight little hole clamped around his cock, and she screamed.

Oh, sweet bliss, she screamed loud enough to make him harder inside of her.

With a smile on his face, he closed his eyes, letting the sounds of their suffering wind around his spine with delicious pleasure.

The night was just beginning, and there'd be so much more to come.

20

VOSS

An entire week somehow slips by uneventfully. Each day, I divide the hours between watching Nola, and popping in to check on Harvey and Beth's place. The white van hasn't come, or gone, in over a week, and every night Nola has walked to her car without incident. No notes, or grisly pictures of victims without eyeballs. As if things have died down.

I know better. It's the calm before the storm. Carl's biding his time, probably watching me, as much as I'm watching out for him.

By now, he has to know where to find me, but he hasn't bothered to pay a visit. Doesn't surprise me, really. Everything he does is meticulously thought out, and no doubt, my part in his game has yet to be revealed.

That's the thing about psychopaths. You don't see them coming until it's too late. Unfortunately for him, I'm not the weak kid he used to know. I've developed an astute sense of detecting death before it strikes.

I knock on the door of the breezeway, where Nola's studio has been the focus of my attention all morning. She's

185

in panic mode, trying to finish a few pieces for her upcoming show, has been all week, hanging out at her potter's wheel, until midnight, most nights.

Meanwhile, I'm in a state of painful arousal after having watched the woman every night. In my daydreams about her, she's covered in wet clay, shiny and glistening, dirty as hell. Sometimes her belly is flat and smooth, sometimes it's bloated with pregnancy, and I don't even want to know why the fuck a visual of that makes me hard. Can't say what it is about her, exactly, that has my body all out of whack, but if I don't fuck something besides my own hand, I'm going to explode with all the pent-up tension.

It's another hour before Oliver gets home from school. An hour I've decided to torment myself by getting closer to her. Taunting myself with the possibilities.

Hands covered in wet clay, she answers the door with a smile. "Voss, what's up?"

In a week, it seems we've grown more comfortable with each other. Whatever reservations she had about me in the beginning have waned, unless she's just become better about hiding it. We smile at each other in passing. Talk with the same cordiality of longtime neighbors. Only, she's the hot neighbor I've fantasized about banging to a pulp.

"Just thought I'd pop in and see what you're up to, *Star Wars*." Bullshit. The only thing popping right now is my zipper, with my dick pressed against it like the bastard might break through any minute.

"C'mon in. I'm just getting ready to wedge."

"Wedge?"

"Yeah, if you don't move the clay around a bit, it gets air pockets. No *bueno*."

"I see." I look around, as if to take in all the pottery, but really, I'm thinking how incredible it'd be to fuck her out here with all these windows. Our own little art exhibition.

"So, where is this art show?"

"Marriott. Why, you want to stop by while I'm there?"

"Maybe." My gaze falls on her again, the way her round ass sticks out from the apron in those tight jeans that I want to cut away with a sharp pair of scissors. I'll bet the muscles she's built, waiting all those tables every day, keep it at a firm bounce that'd feel solid in the palm. And her breasts aren't huge, but just big enough to fill a tight grip, yet small enough to maneuver around. Two weeks, I've gone without sex, and everything about the woman has become some unspoken invitation.

Aside from having a body that taunts me at every turn, her face glows when she's out here. As much as these little deadlines and pressure points she puts herself under stress her out, this room makes her happy.

Holding a thin wire stretched between her hands, she cuts through a block of clay wrapped in a plastic bag, and throws a small square of it down on the table. With the heel of her hand, she rolls it away from her, hips hitting the edge of the table with every push, in a rocking motion that toys with my head.

"This is wedging?" I ask, mesmerized by the act.

"This is wedging," she answers with a smile that'd seal the deal if we were in a bar right now. The soft feminine grunt in her chest, as she toils, strums my desires like prey plucking at a spider's web. "Would you like to try?"

"Try what?"

Chuckling, she shakes her head, pushing the heel of her palm into the clay. "*Wedging*."

Playing with her is effortless. Dare I say, fun. It makes me wonder if she'd be so good-humored while tied to a cross, or laid out across my lap. A million responses roll through my head while I watch her work the clay, imagining her seated reverse cowgirl, with her hands tied behind her back. Those thoughts beckon me closer, and I approach her from behind, caging her against the table.

"Oh, Voss … I was …. I was going to let you have your own."

I press against her harder. "I don't want my own. I want yours."

Her back stiffens at my chest, and if she didn't have a clue how much this little show was turning me on before, she does now.

"Show me first." I bring my arms around hers, taking in the feel of her small body against mine, and I damn near shiver at the many ways I could have this woman. How easy and pliable she'd be. Threading my hands through hers, I can't possibly get any closer, and that's when I feel her tremble against me. Whether from fear, or excitement, I can't tell, and it doesn't matter because my body's on autopilot right now.

I let her guide my hands over the clay, and with each thrust, I crush her between the table and me.

She doesn't stop, or push me away.

Resting my forehead against her nape, I inhale her scent and press my lips to her shoulder. "I want you."

"Voss …" For a moment, I think she's going to deny me, but instead, she spins around, and I hoist her up onto the table, shoving the chunk of clay aside. Hands gripping either side of my face, she pulls me in.

Her lips on mine are heaven, a sweet flavor I've never tasted before.

She's intoxicating.

For the first time in my life, I feel as if I've won this level of attention, not with money, or deals. But by earning her trust.

I work the buttons of her flannel shirt between kisses, exposing the thin lace bra beneath. Peeling back the cup of it,

I take a moment to admire her round, fleshy globes with perfect pink nipples, before leaning forward to suck one of them into my mouth. Fingernails digging into my head, she moans, pressing me against her chest.

Taking her thighs in hand at either side of me, I yank her to the edge of the table and press my neglected dick where I need it, grinding myself into her pussy. Savoring the seconds before I drop trou and plow into her.

Her hand snakes around my neck, the clay getting on my skin and in my hair, but I couldn't give two fucks about that.

"Voss—"

My lips cut her off, sealing her protest with a kiss, but the distant slam of a door snaps both of us out of it.

Real quick.

"Oh, shit!" She glances down at her watch and wriggles against me, until her feet touch the floor again. With hasty fingers, she buttons up her shirt cockeyed, and in smoothing back the mess of her hair, streaks clay over her skin. "Jonah. He's picking up Oliver for the night. I forgot he was stopping by early."

Licking my lips, I will myself to step away from her, to give her space. "You're driving me crazy, woman. These flannel shirts and jeans. You're the ultimate MILF."

"Yeah, well, your suits don't exactly make it easy to look away, either." She drops gaze from mine with a solemn smile.

"Hey-de-ho …" The unfamiliar voice withers, as I turn to see a blond-haired guy, about my height, standing at the door. The same face I saw nearly a week ago, while scoping out Beth and Harv's place. His eyes flick from me to Nola, and back to me.

In the seconds that follow, I wonder if he'll admit to recognizing me. If there's any trace of familiarity that might cause Nola to question everything I've told her about me.

"Jonah. Hi. Um … this is Voss. Well, Rhett Voss. My neighbor."

His brows wing up, and he takes a step toward me, offering a hand. "Nice to meet you."

Cops have always gotten in the way of my work, whether by trying to uphold justice, or traipsing the line of corruption, so as my eyes remain locked on his badge, I'm contemplating where Jonah falls. If he'll be a roadblock, keeping me from my prize in the end. The cock-block to my vengeance.

"Voss? What's wrong?" Nola asks from behind, her question breaking my thoughts.

I lift my hands, completely covered in clay, and smile back at him. "My apologies. Don't mean to be rude."

"I see my sister has indoctrinated you into her clay play."

A quick glance over my shoulder brings Nola's blush-stained face into view, along with her shirt still buttoned wrong, and I wink just before she drops her gaze toward the floor. Swinging my attention back to Jonah, I smile. "Clay play is fast becoming my favorite pastime."

His eyes turn suspicious, as though he's just catching on to what's going on, and he looks past me, to where Nola's standing. "Is that … clay in your hair?"

"It's my fault," I answer for her. "Think I got the clay a little too wet and made a mess. I'll catch you later, Jonah."

"Yeah, okay. Nice to finally meet you uh … Rhett?"

"Voss is fine."

"Voss." He gives a sharp nod and steps aside to let me pass.

"Later, *Nola*."

Her cheeks haven't recovered when she glances up, still holding that beautiful glow of humiliation. "See ya, Voss."

I make a mental note of how perfect she'd look beneath me, face just as flush with all the dopamine and serotonin of climax racing through her blood. My head is still spinning with those visuals when I arrive back at the door of my apart-ment, and I don't immediately notice the note plastered there until it's smacking me in the face.

You steal my pussy, I steal yours.

Slamming through the door, I search my apartment for Vince, my blood pumping with the kind of fury that has me wanting to punch my fist through the goddamn wall.

"Vince! C'mon, buddy." I make the kissy sound that typi-cally has him running from whatever room he's ventured into, but there's no sign of him. "Vince!"

Having searched the place, I race back out onto the small deck, eyes scanning the surrounding trees and yard for any sign of the rotten prick who took him. Must've broken into my apartment while I was preoccupied with Nola.

Like a slap in the face, it's a reminder of why I can't let her get under my skin. My hands ball into fists at my side, crushing the note in my palm. If anything happens to the cat, I'll personally skin Carl alive.

Nabbing my phone from my pocket, I call Jackson, slam-ming the door behind me.

He answers on the third ring. "Yeah, Boss."

"I want everything you can find, everything the police know, about The Sandman killer."

"You get the file I sent a few weeks back?"

Yeah, his anemic file produced nothing more than what the media has reported on the asshole. Mediocre information.

"I want everything, Jackson. FBI reports, missing persons reports, everything you can get your fingers on. *Capisce?*"

"I'll see what I can do."

"Good. Report back to me in the morning."

"Ahh, c'mon, Voss. I've got plans tonight, man."

"Fucking cancel. The cocksucker stole my cat. Everything you can find by morning."

"Ten-four."

I click off the phone, breathing hard through my nose to calm the anger. I've got one more call to make, and unfortunately, I don't think Nola's going to appreciate this one much.

The game has just been ratcheted up a notch.

21

NOLA

"Please. Stop." Hand on my hip, I shake my head and turn to finish wedging the clay, desperately trying to ignore my brother's prying stare.

"I'm just saying. There's something off about him. Maybe he's a decent guy, but something isn't right." Jonah plops into a chair across from me and crosses his arms.

"You said you'd come over early to give me the scoop on Beth and Harv. So, why are we talking about Voss?"

"A week ago, I swung by their place, as you asked me to. While I was there, someone was inside the house."

"Who? Did you see him?"

"No. The guy jumped through a window and took off. I'd have put out a search for him, but technically, I wasn't even supposed to be in that house without a warrant, and I suppose, it could've been one of them."

"So, what does this have to do with Voss?"

"You said he scared Harvey off that night in the parking lot. Any chance he'd have a connection with the two?"

Knowing Beth, she'd certainly *try* to make a connection

with Voss, but I doubt she'd get anywhere with him. Just a guess, but he seems to like a bit of chase. "Like what?"

"I don't know. You said the two of them like to swing."

"I said no such thing."

"Okay, Diane told me. So what. You told her."

"Are you implying that Voss had sex with them?" The thought of kissing Beth's sloppy seconds is enough to make me gag, even if it isn't likely.

"I'm trying to make a connection. I'm also trying to figure out who the hell was in that house."

"Well, it wasn't Voss. He's had a number of opportunities to … hurt me, and hasn't. And I don't think there's a connection to Harvey, either. The guy does nice things, but he's not the type to go all vigilante after Harvey for leaving twisted little love notes. He's not like that."

"Like what?"

"He just … he's not a …"

"Good guy?"

"No. I mean, yes. He's … kinda half and half. He doesn't go out of his way, but when he does, he's very sweet. Kinda bad, secretly good."

"And you're attracted to this?"

I freeze at that, clearing my throat as I press the heels of my hands into the clay. "What? What … what makes you think that? I didn't say that."

"Because your face hasn't stopped burning red since I got here."

"You're frustrating me. I like him as a neighbor, okay? He doesn't blare his music, or have women coming and going every day. He's just a quiet guy who values his privacy."

"You just described about half the killers in state prison."

"Can you just tell me what you have on Beth and Harv, please?"

"I've asked around. Neighbors. Some of the bars they

apparently hang out in. Beth hasn't been active on her social media account in the last week."

"So? I haven't been on mine in over a year. Doesn't mean I'm dead in a ditch."

"No, but she's far more involved than you ever were. Some interesting groups she follows."

"Yeah. She's weird. We know this. So, what happens at this point?"

"Dale reported her missing, so the two of them are in the system. I'll keep you updated if I hear anything, but I'm not going to lie, Nola. There's not much we can do with adults. Overall, there doesn't seem to be any overwhelming evidence of foul play. *Technically*, they're allowed to disappear. It's not a crime for them not to show up at work, or slack off on their social media posts. But my bigger concern is the note you received from Harvey. He has a record of harassment, so I'm advising you to watch yourself and call either myself, or the station, if he tries to contact you again."

Lips pursed, I wipe my hands on my apron and offer a nod. "Yeah, sure."

"I'm serious, Nola. You know, it's bad enough you work these late hours. Some days, I wish I could lock you up just to keep you safe."

"That'd be sibnapping and I'm pretty sure it's just as illegal as kidnapping."

"You're not even serious about it. That's the worst part."

"I am serious." Picking the clay from my nails, I half smile. "Look, I know why you do this, Jonah. Why you're so dedicated to finding this guy who's kidnapping these girls. I know … you're just … watching out for me."

The troubled look on his face sends my stomach into knots, because it's coming. I brought it up and planted the seed in his head and now he's going to drag me back through those memories. It's how we torture ourselves, Jonah and me.

When one brings it up, the other is tasked with punishment so we don't forget her.

Shaking his head, he crosses his arms over his chest. "I remember the night Nora went missing. The look on Dad's face. All my life, I saw him as this invincible man who took down the bad guys. My own personal Superman. And I realized in that moment, he wasn't invincible at all. Even Superman had a weakness."

"She might've run away, you know. She might still be alive." Even my belief in that has shriveled a bit through the years. Why wouldn't Nora try to contact the two of us?

"Maybe so. That doesn't make it any easier to accept."

"It doesn't."

The door slams again, alerting us that Oliver is home from school. A minute later, he enters the studio, backpack slung over his shoulder.

"There he is! Muhammed Oli!" Jonah snaps from his somber face like he switched the channel from emo to pop, and he hops to his feet, pretending to spar with Oliver.

His memory of Dad still twists inside my gut, but I chuckle at the Ali reference and wait for them to finish goofing off.

Oliver's eye has healed significantly over the week, turning to a yellowish bruise, and I've not had any issues getting him up for school since that Monday.

"Your eye is lookin' good, man. All packed for tonight?"

Oliver nods and glances over at me, since I was the one who packed his bag this morning.

"Everything's in there. Earbuds, books, broccoli and Brussels sprouts."

With a roll of his eyes, Oli snorts, and makes his way over to me. His arms wrap around me, and my heart damn near stops right there.

Hands hanging loose at my sides, I have to tell myself to

hug him back, or risk him pulling away in some unrequited show of emotion. Tears gather in my eyes while I hold him to me.

It's been months since he last showed me affection like this, without my prodding him to, and I almost don't know how to respond anymore.

When he pulls away, he raises his hands between us and signs *I love you.*

All those months of him basically ignoring his ASL teacher, and he pulls this shit now, of all times? When I'm already beating myself up at the idea that I'm sending him off again?

Damn it, I can't help the tears.

I echo his sign and kiss the top of his head. "Be good. I love you, Oliver."

With a nod and a sheepish smile that borders on embarrassment, he heads back into the house.

"We'll see you after your show tomorrow, then?" Jonah asks.

Wiping my eyes on my shoulder, I force a smile, as Jonah bends forward to kiss my cheek. "Tomorrow. Thanks Jonah. For everything."

"Stay out of trouble." He lifts his gaze past me toward Voss's apartment in the back, then follows after Oliver.

R ubbing the knot in my neck, I dip my toe into the bathwater, shivering with anticipation of the toasty temperature that hits my skin, and step inside. The heat washes over me like a cozy blanket, and I settle back against the curved basin. In less than a minute, the tension in my muscles sizzles away, and I close my eyes, breathing in the thick steam that coats the back of my throat.

Tipping my head back, I submerge my ears to just below the water, muting out the rest of the house, and my thoughts drift to earlier in the evening, with Jonah. His comments about Voss.

Jonah's always had pretty sound judgment when it comes to people, but I can't help thinking he's wrong about my neighbor. Sure, Voss is quiet, maybe even borderline asshole, at times, but he's not a bad guy. Not from what I've seen, anyway.

And I've seen quite a bit of him. His body pressed into mine earlier today was a reminder that he's not the kind of man who minces words when it comes to what he wants. It's obvious he came to visit me for one thing, and I can't say that turns me off. We've had this maddening dance of tension for the past week now, with our little niceties that leave each encounter feeling open-ended. As if there should be more.

The two of us are like day and night, though—light and darkness. And his sexual prowess scares me a bit, because I'm certain the man is far more experienced with women who are far more practiced in things he likes.

I'm just a mom with a soft belly and a C-section scar.

Voss is virility in the flesh, with a body made for sex, and a voice that's equally arousing. The mere thought of those muscles he hides beneath his fancy suits, covered in tattoos, flexing and contracting in slow, controlled movements is enough to make me squeeze my thighs together. Those intense eyes staring back at me, the right flanked by a scar that tells me someone, or something, tried to hurt him once, and failed.

How shamelessly those eyes would consume a woman, like thunderstorms tearing across a tranquil landscape. The last thing she'd see, before blinding pleasure strikes in a snap of wicked lightning. He'd undoubtedly leave any woman soaked and shaken afterward.

Stop it, Nola.

It's been six months since my husband's death, and I'm already fantasizing about a man. A complete stranger, no less. I screw my eyes shut to stamp out the thoughts of Voss, and whatever little sexual metaphors he conjures, in my head. I have a son to focus on, and my pottery show coming up. I don't need to be indulging in these wet daydreams.

It's just that he's big and imposing. Dominant. The complete opposite of Denny. Voss is a man who takes control, takes what he wants.

A flash of him ripping away my panties has me gripping the edge of the tub to keep my hands away from my thighs.

I will not get myself off to this man. Regardless of the fact that we nearly got it on this afternoon, the fact is, Voss is off limits. He's my tenant. My neighbor. A business transaction.

Forbidden.

Which makes him more enticing, somehow.

Smooth porcelain glides across my ass as I squirm with the visuals of him sneaking into my house, and up into my bathroom, watching me bathe right now. I spread my thighs apart, imagining his hands doing the same, as if he's in this cramped tub with me. A dark stranger with a single agenda.

Palms on my knees, he holds me open, and I kick out at him to get away, but one strong yank captures me. Water splashes over the edge of the bath as he wrangles me beneath him, his big body caging me in so there's no hope for escape.

My fingers tingle with the urge to touch the ache between my thighs, but I can't. I won't get myself off to these thoughts that border on forced sex. Growing up in a sexually-repressed house as a teenager, I often had these darker sort of fantasies, ones that allowed me to indulge without the guilt of actually enjoying something so perverse. To sate my desires without the punishment of my conscience. Unfortunately, my mother further smothered my curiosities, by making it clear that masturbation was something to be ashamed about, something only a person constantly preoccupied with sex would do.

I was always taught women who craved sex were little *trollops,* as I recall my mother saying, when she found out my father had been propositioned by one—his secretary. She'd have been horrified to know, as a freshman in high school, I sometimes touched myself to thoughts of senior Jake Northcott ravaging me in his dad's pickup truck. The twisted imaginations of a young girl pining for the captain of the football team, but it wasn't always confined to just him. Sometimes, my fantasies took place in the locker room with the other players, all of them wanting a turn with the shy and quiet Stiever girl.

So wrong.

Yet, something about those sinister little scenarios excites me. The chase. The dominance.

My ultimate surrender.

I imagine Voss pushing himself inside me, anesthetizing me with his dark poison. Hammering his hips into me while he whispers dirty things in my ear. Terrifying truths that keep me on edge, as he toys with my limits. *You love this, don't you, Nola?*

God, he'd feel so good. Railing into me, while he watches me come apart at the seams, unraveling all my tightly-knitted control, until I'm lying in messy spools of what I once was.

I ball my hands into fists, as the visual overwhelms my senses, pervading every dark corner of my mind. *Stop.* I have more important things to ponder, after all, but his hands on my body this afternoon left behind phantom reminders of how good it feels to be touched by a man.

Particularly one as dominant and arousing as Voss.

The water splashes around me in celebration of my

frenzy, as my body tenses, begging for one single touch, one quick climax.

I can't.

"Ah!" A knot in my belly pulls tighter, until I'm rubbing my ass against the porcelain with these wicked thoughts of Voss.

Voss.

Even his name is sex on my tongue. Perhaps because it rhymes so well with *boss*, and that's exactly how I imagine him with me right now. Taking charge. Unfettered by guilt and shame, or anything that gets in the way of his pleasure.

"You love when I fuck you," the imaginary Voss says. *"Admit it."*

The strings pull, winding my muscles up, and I can't take it anymore.

One touch. That's it.

Just one.

The second my fingers make contact with my clit, my body seizes as though shocked with gratification. In a few quick caresses, a wave of heat blasts through me, prickling my veins with a powerful release.

"Voss!" The sound of his name reverberates against the empty bathroom walls, an echo of ecstasy that sends one more shot of rapture through my body.

Muscles weak and flaccid, I open my mouth to catch my breath and settle into the tub again. The water goes still around me.

It's been a long time since I felt that level of satisfaction from a fantasy. A long time since I've gotten myself off with such intensity that I'm exhausted from it. I can't even imagine how it'd feel in real life.

Breathing slow and easy, I bring my legs together and curl my toes.

I won't do it again, I promise myself.

I can't.

R ose colored powder dusts the white porcelain sink, as Nora flicks the wide brush over her cheeks. With olive skin, blonde hair, and long black lashes set above beautiful chestnut eyes, she doesn't need makeup. Still, the bright red lipstick is striking, mesmerizing, as I focus on her lips.

"You're staring." Her tone is flat and teasing, and the second I make eye contact, her signature dimple makes an appearance with a playful smile. "Stop."

"What's his name?" I rest my chin on my elbow I've propped against the edge of the bathtub, while I soak in steamy water.

"Brian. He's a physiology major."

"What's that?"

"He wants to be a sports doctor someday, so he studies body function."

"Thought you said athletes were boneheads."

She chuckles and drags a brush, dipped in black mascara, over her eyelashes. "Most of them are. But Brian is ... different. I think you'd like him."

The age gap between me and my siblings is enough that I'm sometimes mistaken for her daughter—an error that I secretly appreciate, but I wouldn't tell my mother that. Nora doesn't look anything like my mother did when she was nineteen, but everyone says I will someday. My mother was beautiful back then, so it isn't an insult.

Nora, on the other hand, takes after my father, with her sandy blonde hair and big bright eyes.

"Help me?" Crouching beside the tub, Nora turns her back to me, holding the two ends of the gold necklace our father bought her for Christmas. Its pendant is dual circles joined *together to form an infinity. I have one, too, only mine is sitting on the sink so I don't lose it in the bathtub.*

I clasp the ends together for her, careful not to get bathwater on her shirt. "What do I tell Mom?"

Our parents went out for their weekly bowling date, leaving Nora in charge. Even though she's nineteen, my parents are pretty strict with my sister. They feel that, because they're paying for her education, her focus should be on her studies. Not boys. For the last six years of her life, it has, so I have to believe there's something special about this boy, for her to risk my father's wrath.

"I should be home before they get back. But if I'm not, tell them I crashed while studying for exams. I'll stuff some pillows under my bedspread before I go."

"I hate lying to them. I wish he'd just cut you some slack."

"You and me, both, sister."

She pecks me on the forehead and smiles. "I was watching Jonah when I was your age." A gentle stroke over my wet hair, and she tucks a loose strand behind my ear. "You're practically an adult."

"Be careful, okay?"

"I will. Quit fretting. It's just a date. We're not going off to elope."

It wouldn't surprise me if she did, though. My parents have always been so much harder on her. I don't think they mean to. I just think they recognize the potential in her.

"I lanu!" She bends forward and kisses me on the cheek. It's a joke between us. When I was a baby, and my mother would try to get me to say 'I love you' to Nora, I always somehow combined her name with the words, and it's stuck ever since.

"I lanu, too." I chuckle, and roll back into the water, until my ears are below the surface and the world is mute, and I close my eyes.

Distant sounds reach my ear. Screaming. My eyes flip open to my sister's face, scrunched in anger as she stands over me. Red

*lipstick streaks across her cheeks like blood. Black mascara
streams down from her eyes like a scary clown's.*

"*Why did you lie, Nola?*"

My heart races, my stomach turns with nausea.

"*Why did you lie!*"

I shoot up to a sitting position, splashing water over the
edge of the tub, and gasp. Glancing around the bathroom
shows no sign of Nora anywhere. Not that it would. Through
deep inhalations, I slow my breathing and shutter my eyes,
burying my face into my knees. The bath water has gone ice
cold, only adding to the chill that clings to my bones, and
the chattering of my teeth marks the incessant vibrations
running below my skin.

Seventeen years. It's been seventeen years, and her disappearance still haunts me.

With Denny's murder, as horrific as it was, I, at least, had
closure. And anger, to keep me from drowning in the guilt.
The remorse I carried didn't hold a candle to the agony of
that night, when my sister didn't come home and my parents
asked me where she'd gone.

I lied and told them I didn't know, because for one brief
moment, I thought *maybe* she had run away to elope. *Maybe*
she'd fallen in love with Brian and skipped off to wedded
bliss with him. Away from my parents. Away from the
responsibilities that always bogged her down.

I had no idea that wasn't how love worked. Had I known
she would never make it to Brian's house, that he'd spend
that night angry at the girl he thought had stood him up,
that every second I lied and told my parents I didn't know
where she'd gone, was another second she might've been
given to return. Had I known all these things, I might've
begged her not to go that night. I might've called my parents
and told them straight away where she'd gone.

I might've been the good daughter.

Instead, I lay in my bed that night, silent and happy and so ignorant about love, believing some twisted fairytale, in which my sister had ridden off with her white knight. I quietly laughed at my parents' stupidity, thinking how sorry they'd be when they found out she hadn't pursued vet medicine, and instead, chose love, just like in the stories Nora made up at bedtime.

The joke was on me, though, when police came to the door. When I watched my dad collapse because they couldn't find my sister, and her boyfriend didn't know where she was, either. When that fairytale twisted into something more sinister, and the questions began to mount inside my head.

It's no wonder I couldn't say the word as a child. I never truly grasped the meaning of love.

Nor, even, when I became an adult.

22

NOLA

The craft show is at the Mariott in downtown, and as I wheel in the cart holding all my wares, I take note of the strange costumes first. Everyone's wearing black. Black capes. Black makeup. Black everything. My table is next to a heavier-set woman, positioning candles and black satchels on her table, and little necklace thingies she refers to as talismans.

This should be my first clue, really, but I'm so preoccupied with the thought that half my sets aren't *full* sets, I don't notice the symbols and signs and everything that serves as a marquee for my idiocy. No, it isn't until someone asks me what power my ceramics hold, and if I sell a mortar and pestle, that I realize craft is short for *witch*craft.

A fucking witchcraft convention.

Hands covering my face, I burst into laughter when it hits me, to the point of tears, and the stares I draw aren't friendly.

This is, by far, the only way I can possibly imagine this week ending.

A woman steps up to my booth, and when she asks me if

I happen to sell cauldrons, a howl of laughter escapes me, sending her off to my neighbor.

I must look possessed, with bouts of uncontrollable cackling.

Who the hell mistakes a witchcraft convention for a craft show, after all?

"How's it going, *Star Wars*?" The deep velvet voice quiets my amusement, and when I slide my hands from my face, Voss is standing in front of me. In a three-piece suit that clings to his muscles, he's almost enough distraction to keep me from breaking down.

"Look around and tell me who, in this place, doesn't belong?" Another spasm of laughter bursts from my chest, and when his gaze trails over the surrounding booths and back to me, his lips stretch with a smile.

"Well, you got the craft part right, anyway."

A wheeze brings more tears to my eyes, which I wipe away. "I haven't sold a damn thing!" More laughter.

Voss chuckles, too, the sound of his amusement only adding to mine.

Until it hits me. All this work, and I'm a hundred bucks in the hole for the table fee. A hundred bucks that I'd rather have spent on Oli for Christmas. A hundred bucks I could've used to pay a bill, or take him out to dinner. A hundred bucks I just donated to a bunch of witches.

Suddenly, it isn't so funny anymore.

"How much for everything?" Voss's question breaks me out of my silent lamenting.

"What?"

"How much would you have made had you sold everything?"

I shrug, not really wanting to think about it, since the number is so far away at the moment. "Eight hundred. Give, or take."

"All that work for eight hundred? You're selling yourself short, Nola." He picks up one of the vases I repaired, with its golden cracks over shiny black glaze. "I'll give you a thousand for everything. Do you ship?"

"Very funny, Voss. That's as bad as Jonah coming in here to buy all my shit."

"My apartment is lacking. I could use some hand-thrown pottery."

"Okay, I'll *give* you a few vases, but I'm not selling to you."

"Is it because we're neighbors?"

"Is that all we are still? I was wondering about that after yesterday."

His brow wings up and he glances over his shoulder, his head obviously spinning with more ideas than mine at the moment. "If you didn't have the burden of needing money, would you give this stuff away?"

"Ah, is this a test to see how passionate I am about pottery?"

He shrugs and stuffs his hands into his perfectly pressed slacks. "Maybe I'm just trying to get rid of this shit so I can take you out to dinner."

"I guess I'd give it away, if someone wanted it. It'd be nice not to have to cart all this stuff home again."

He tugs his wallet from his pocket and counts out a thousand dollars in front of me, then turns to face the crowd. "Excuse me! Can I have your attention?"

The crowd ignores him, the noise of witches shopping too loud for him to be heard.

Using the chair set out for me, he climbs up onto my table, leaving me staring at shiny, polished black shoes that I can practically see my reflection in.

"Voss! What are you doing?"

"Excuse me! Can I have your attention?" The conversations die down, and all eyes turn toward Voss.

Once again, my cheeks are burning. Hot.

"For the next ten minutes, everything at this table is free to take!"

The second he announces it, the sound of pounding hits my ears, as a stampede makes their way to my table. Women and men dressed in black capes and hats, fighting over my pottery like it's Black Friday at Walmart. The table wiggles and jostles. Someone knocks over a now-empty wooden crate that once housed a stack of dishes. The Christmas tree I set out for display lies tipped over on the table, it's mini bulbs rolling around in front of me.

It doesn't even take ten minutes for every piece of pottery on my table to disappear, along with my business cards and the bowl of mints I set out.

My table is empty, as ravaged as a tuna buffet in a piranha tank.

And for the second time today, I break into hysterical laughter.

I wheel a single box, filled mostly with table props, out of the conference room and find Voss waiting for me by the elevator. In his arms is a small crate with a table cloth, lights, and gift bags that nobody bothered to use. "I don't know whether to hate you, or hug you, right now."

"Tell me you wanted to sit through Pixie's seminar on Potions, and I'll feel like shit for what I did."

My stomach can't possibly muster another laugh, but it does. And when the elevator dings, opening up to more witches, I clamp my mouth shut, feeling as if I'm about to explode when I step inside.

"'Nough said," Voss says, the serious tone of his voice sending me over the edge.

My head hurts from laughing so much, or maybe it's just the exhaustion of having gotten my ass up early to set up for this. "Part of me wants to cry. I can't believe I did this." I press the button to the garage level, about twelve floors down from the conference room, and rest my head against the mirrored wall.

"Well, that'll teach you to read the fine print, won't it?"

"You didn't have to do that back there. I feel like you've rescued me more times this week than anyone has my whole life."

He sets the basket on the floor of the elevator and crowds me against the wall. "Stay with me."

"What?"

"I'll get a room. We'll get some wine. Fuck all night."

My spine vibrates with a chill, and I mentally swallow the visual he's planted in my head. "Voss … I have … I have to pick up Jonah. I mean, Oliver. From Jonah's."

"Three hours, *Star Wars*. That's all I want." He toys with a curl in my hair, smoothing the strand between his fingers. "Three hours with you. Alone."

"I don't …"

Palm cupping my jaw, he crushes his lips to mine, the spicy cinnamon of his breath only adding to the delicious taste in my mouth. Voss doesn't just kiss, he consumes, engulfing me in his heat. What began as a tiny spark of excitement in my fingertips catches flame inside me and moves through my veins as if to burn through every ounce of my resistance. "Three hours. Please."

The husky tone of his voice bleeds a small bit of desperation, like every minute counts against him.

"Voss. Do you think that's a good idea?"

The elevator dings, and he steps aside, when it opens to

the sixth floor and an older woman walks on. She smiles and turns her back to us, the awkward silence broken by the gasp that escapes me, when Voss snakes his hand down my ass and between my thighs.

The woman turns to smile again and clears her throat, before returning her attention toward the numbers counting down the floors.

Fingertips dancing across the sensitive skin between my legs, he fondles me in the most deliciously forbidden way. Every nerve in my body hums as the pad of his finger traces closer across my skin to the thin fabric separating him from what he's made clear he wants most.

He finds it, reaching lower, until he's probing the entrance, warning me of what's to come.

Literally.

Lips parted, I close my eyes, mentally willing myself not to breathe too harshly. Not to get too caught up in the fantasies of being fingered right here in public, behind some poor, unsuspecting lady who has no idea how wicked this man is.

As if he read my mind last night in the bathtub. I'm dizzy with want, and his touch is selling exactly what I need right now.

"Three hours," he whispers, but certainly not quiet enough for what he's doing to me. "Deal?"

"Shhhh!"

The older woman clears her throat a second time.

Running his finger up and down my slit, he kisses the shell of my ear. "If you don't, my dick will fall off, and I'll spend the rest of my life masturbating with a pillow."

Hand slapped to my face, I try to cap the snort that escapes me, and my body convulses with silent laughter.

"Please. Do it for the pillows." He smiles against my cheek and bites at my earlobe, which truth be told, only adds to the dizzy sensation from before. "Will you stay with me?"

"What's the significance of three hours?" I whisper, and goddamn, this elevator is taking forever.

"You'll have to stay with me to find out." The moment his fingers break contact, the knot in my stomach eases, and the wetness he's stoked saturates my cotton panties until they're sliding against my skin.

The elevator dings again, opening to the lobby, and before the older woman in front of us exits, she turns around, setting her hand on my arm, and leans in. "Life's short, sweetheart. Rent the room. For the sake of pillows everywhere." With a wink, she hobbles away.

Eyes wide with horror, I thump my fist into Voss's shoulder. The door closes again, and he grabs either side of my face, backing me into the wall.

His tongue dips past my teeth, deepening his kiss, and he drags my thigh up over his hip. With my knee hiked, he once again has access to what he wants, and the tickle along my slit is a warning. "I want more, Nola."

The elevator dings and opens to the lower level, where the garage sits beneath the hotel. No one there, not that it seems to matter to Voss, who keeps on with his curious tongue and wandering fingers. It closes again, but doesn't move.

We do, though. Voss drags his lips down over my throat, biting my jawline along the way. I'm squirming in his solid arms like a worm caught on a hook. Frantic and impatient, we tear into each other like it's the last few seconds on earth.

"I'll do anything to make you mine tonight. Anything you want." Pushing the crotch of my damp panties aside, he flicks his finger over my sodden entrance and shudders a breath. "Fuck, you're already wet for me."

"You can have … any woman. Why me? I'm just … just a mom."

"You're a hot mom. A beautiful mom. And I got fucking mommy issues." Only the tip of his finger slips inside. In and out, bringing to mind a stark awareness that it's been too long. Too long since I've felt wanted. Desired.

Properly fucked.

Trollop. I cringe at the words of my mother. But then I remember, my mother had a man who doted on her for years, and she never once appreciated him. She never felt the empty void of affection, never spent her nights trying to remember the scent of her husband, or the sound of his voice. She built her own cage to avoid my father, to shun his affections, so she wouldn't know the first thing about what I need right now.

"Three hours. That's it, right?"

"Three hours."

I don't know what the hell is so significant about three hours, but I reach out and press the button for the lobby. "Okay. Deal."

"I had no idea you could pay for a hotel room with cash."

"You can do just about anything, if you talk to the right person." Voss threads his fingers in mine, stepping aside for the wait staff, who wheel in dinner and two of their best bottles of wine, per his request. I catch him slip a wad of green into the waiter's palm as he passes, and the moment he closes the door, my heart flutters like it's prom night all over again.

A whirlpool tub takes up the corner of the room across from the bed. Not in the bathroom. Across from the bed. As if to encourage sex afterward. To the right of it stands a wide dresser mirror that takes up half the wall, beyond the foot of the bed, offering a clear, unobstructed view. Like voyeurs. The whole damn room seems to be designed for one thing.

I can't even turn around for fear I'll end up doing something embarrassing, like passing out. The last time I was with a guy, other than Denny, was Spin-The-Bottle at age fourteen, when Jake Northcott pulled me into a closet to kiss me.

The age gap between Voss and me is suddenly apparent, as I stand here, feeling like an inexperienced girl, against this man who's probably had a woman every way imaginable. I don't even know what's sexy anymore. I'm only glad that I wore matching underwear and shaved my legs during my bath the night before.

"Turn around, Nola." He's closer now. Close enough that I can feel the buzz of excitement vibrating off of him.

With a deep breath, I turn around to catch him unbuttoning his shirt, and everything comes crashing in on me with vivid reality. This is really happening.

"Take your panties off," he says, popping his cufflinks.

The tickle of his command beats against my skin like a soft caress, and I steal a minute to focus on my breathing. *Take your panties off.* My stomach flutters, sending goosebumps across my flesh. His words reverberate inside my head, telling me there's no going back to just Voss and Nola after this. Taking off my panties will be lowering my guard, letting down the walls and leaving myself open and vulnerable to whatever Voss has in mind.

Taking a moment to release a shaky exhale, I reach around for the zip of my skirt, only loosening the small latch, before he pauses his undressing.

"Not the skirt. Just the panties."

"Just the panties," I echo, abandoning the zipper. Part of me is relieved I get to shield some part of myself, but another part of me says that isn't how Voss works. Somehow, even with my skirt on, this will undoubtedly be the dirtiest experience I've ever had.

He slowly peels his shirt over thick shoulders, exposing the lean, cut muscle of his body beneath as if he's preparing me for a fight.

If that's the case, his body is a momentary distraction of pure perfection—one that has me mentally calibrating our compatibility. Will that body hurt me? If he's as proportionate as what I've seen so far, I'm in trouble.

A patch of white draws my attention to a bandage taped across his bicep. "What happened there?" I ask, tipping my head toward it.

He doesn't even bother to look, as if far too distracted to care. "Nothing. Unbutton your shirt, and take off your bra."

What is it with him, making me undress beneath my clothes like I'm some Houdini master?

The curiosity compels me to find out, so I unfasten the buttons of my shirt, one by one, desperate to remember whether, or not, I put on deodorant this morning.

Meanwhile, Voss unzips his slacks, pushing them down his thighs over hard, chiseled muscles that look strong enough to crush me.

I reach inside my shirt and slide my arms from the loops of my bra, pulling the garment out of my sleeve and letting it fall to the floor.

He corners me, setting a palm to the wall beside my head, like a cunning wolf happening upon a small and unwitting rabbit in the woods. Reaching down between us, he hikes my skirt to just below my bare sex beneath and takes a moment to squeeze the back of my thighs.

In the mirror across from me, I look disheveled. Messy. The embodiment of sexual repression unleashed.

Dragging his fingertip down along the edge of my crisp, white shirt, he grazes my nipple, seeming to study me as he drags it back up for another pass. The sensation of his finger over my diamond hard flesh sends another wet rush between my thighs.

"Stay put."

He crosses the room to the tray that stands beside the small kitchenette, and opens the bottle of wine, popping the cork, before pouring two glasses. Setting the bottle back on the tray, he pauses and lifts what looks to be a long, silicone stopper for the bottle, twisting it around with some unsaid curiosity. A quick glance back at me, and he moves to the sink, pumping a small bit of soap over it, and flips on the faucet.

Washing it?

Instead of pushing the stopper into the bottle, he flips the cork and plugs the opening with it, then returns carrying a glass of wine and the stopper.

Eyes narrowed, I instinctively back up a step. "What are you doing?"

"Drink some wine."

"Not until I know what you plan to do with the wine stopper."

"I plan to fuck you with it, Nola."

I back up another step and frown.

"I'm a bit of a naturalist when it comes to sex. We're surrounded by things—props and toys—that make it so much more exciting. Yet, half the time we don't even use the shit."

"So, you brought me up here to get yourself off, is that it? To get your fucking jollies watching me bang a wine stopper?"

"When was the last time you went outside of your comfort zone?"

"Never. I'm pretty sure that's why they exist, ya know? Boundaries."

"Boundaries exist to box you in. To make you fear what's on the other side of them."

"Boundaries keep others from venturing into places they don't belong." I wriggle my finger toward the stopper. "Keeps you from feeling unnecessary pain."

"No one knows that better than me, Nola." Snorting a laugh, he sets the wine down on the nightstand beside us. Without warning, he slaps his hand to my mouth, his big, imposing body pressing into me, until the wall hits my spine.

The shock tightens my muscles into a strange paralysis, every muscle trembling with adrenaline.

"But let's say, for a second, that you step outside those boundaries," he whispers, and licks his lips. "Say that you make yourself vulnerable for a minute." He twists the stopper in front of me. "What if it felt fucking incredible to let go like that? Could you, in all your tightly-wound up morals and virtues even imagine such a thing?" His eyes are on me, thick with lust and challenge, and I can feel my heartbeat soaring in response. The cool silicone tickles my thigh as he traces it up and down my leg. "You think it's appalling to fuck something so common as a wine stopper. But what if it felt good, Nola? How ashamed would you feel getting off on it?"

Teasing the hem of my skirt with the object, he keeps his hand pressed to my mouth, his warm cinnamon breath beating against my throat, where he drags his tongue, just before his lips clamp down.

"Ah!" My muffled cry arrives as more of a whimper behind the barricade at my mouth.

The stopper trails up my skirt, only grazing my exposed slit. "I'll make a deal with you. Let me fuck you with this, and if you don't come, I'll let you watch me fuck myself with it."

Part of me wants to laugh at such a bold statement. This

man doesn't know as much as he thinks he does about my body to make that kind of a deal.

"Are you willing to go outside your boundaries, Nola?"

The tip of the stopper presses against my seam as he gently draws up and down over my clit. Penetrating gray eyes study me, burning with intrigue and what I surmise to be a small bit of amusement.

My knees turn weak, eyes heavy with a foreign rush, and I nod.

"Good girl." Pressing his knee against my thigh, he spreads my legs as far as the skirt will allow, still pinning me against the wall. Kissing along my jaw, he drags the tip down to my entrance and pauses there, circling it against my flesh, teasing me. My belly is tight with anticipation, my hands balled into fists against the wall at either side of me. "I want to watch you come all over this," he whispers and pushes the stopper up into me.

I gasp against his palm at the unexpected pleasure of the ribs rubbing along my walls, and flex my fingers in an effort to hold onto something. The ridges of the stopper add just enough friction to each glide, and I can't help but moan at the delicious intrusion.

No, it's wrong. This isn't romantic, it's dirty and humiliating, and I tell myself not to be lured by such wicked pleasures my mother always referred to as *carnal* and *unbecoming* when she talked to me about sex.

"It should be pure and discreet, and only between two people who love each other," she often said.

Yet, in seconds, I'm panting against his hand, struggling to keep upright, as the wet sounds betray my resistance. A slap in my mother's face, as my body shivers with each new thrust.

"Listen to that. All your morals falling down. Fucking music to my ears." There's an edge of excitement to his words, a shaky quality in his voice, as he ups the pace, breathing hard against my throat, like he's the one getting off. "Don't you come, *Star Wars*. You wouldn't want to lose the bet."

I moan again, my whole body warring against itself, as he strings me along toward climax.

With every plunge, there's an awareness that I have no chance of winning this, as the stopper becomes increasingly slick from my juices.

"I'm going to fuck you after this. Because I can't stand the thought of not being inside you for one more minute. I'm going to fuck you hard, Nola. And something tells me you'll *like* it," he says through clenched teeth.

Another ripple of ecstasy winds down my spine, and as I slide against the wall, he presses into me, urging me back up.

"No, no. Not until you come." He tugs the stopper out of me and sucks it clean, before reinserting it. "You taste so good." His voice is more ragged, before his tongue curls around my nipple.

I arch, crying out, as he sucks and flicks and bites, moaning against my flesh.

Every part of me begs to reject such an arrogant assumption that I'd enjoy rough sex with him, but I can't. Not after he's already proven me wrong.

Gripping his arm for support, I feel the ball of muscle beneath his skin, the tension running thick through him, telling me he has no intentions of giving in.

I'm deliriously close to climax, so much so, I feel drunk, and when he plunges one last time, my whole body squirms and shudders as a rush of tingles explodes through my muscles. All I can do is mewl against his palm like a trapped little kitten who's fallen prey to the lion.

"That's it, baby. That's what I want to hear."

When my gaze shifts to his, there's a knowing smile on

his face, but without all the smugness. He looks pleased. And for reasons I can't wrap my head around in the moment, I like that. We stare at each other, only the sound of our stuttering breaths filling the quiet between us. I watch the way the muscles in his biceps and chest flex and tighten while he finishes me. Ruins me in ways I wasn't anticipating. How his chest rises and falls quickly with panting breaths that match my own. As if the two of us are completely in sync.

His eyes are hard and concentrated, a thunderstorm that I want to sweep me away. He leans forward, kissing me as he pushes the stopper in and leaves it there. "Get on the bed. Now."

I do as he says, awkwardly hobbling along as the evidence of my arousal trickles down my thighs and the stopper reminds me of why. Midway onto the bed, I turn to see him staring at me in the mirror's reflection. Ass propped, I can see everything—including the glistening bare skin with the wine stopper sticking out of me that betrays every morally questionable thought I've had so far.

Voss moans, and I catch a glimpse of him out of the corner of my eye.

He strokes himself with eyes rapt on me, giving me the perfect view of his fully erect cock sticking up from his muscled thighs. "Beautiful, isn't it? How can a man not want to fuck that?"

Shrinking into myself, I study the width of the mirror's reflection and there's no hiding from it. "I can't do this. Not if I have to watch myself the whole time."

"What's wrong with watching yourself?"

"It's just … weird."

"Out of your comfort zone."

"Way out. Like … across the galaxy."

"Well, that's the point, *Star Wars*." He yanks my legs, and my body slides across the mattress until my ass slams into his thighs. "Hands behind your back."

Knees still weak and muscles warm with fresh climax, I do as he says, and when I hear the tearing of foil, I know this thing between us has only just begun. Lifting my head off the bed, I watch the reflection of him rolling a condom down his shaft.

In the next breath, he buries his face in my ass, and I jerk forward to get away. My God, the idea of his face there is mortifying. My stomach curls with embarrassment as he holds me still, his fingers digging into my hips as he licks my most forbidden place.

"Voss! Wait … please."

He doesn't stop, and in spite of the shame, I roll my head against the mattress, while his tongue sweeps over my hole and down to the stopper. Teeth gripping the edges, he removes the object, spitting it out onto the bed beside me, and sucks at my over-sensitive flesh with the fervor of a man who's been denied water too long. In the mirror, I'm propped face down, with my hands bound behind my back, watching him stroke his cock as he essentially eats me out. I clamp my eyes to shield out the visual that, admittedly, is the most darkly erotic thing I've even seen. It tickles my belly and sends a of rush of blood to my core. I bury my face in the mattress, mouth gaping, moaning, desperate for air and mercy, while his tongue wets my swollen folds, his lips kissing and sucking away my useless protests. The guttural rumble of contentment in his throat reminds me of an animal relishing its recent kill.

Carnal and unbecoming.

If my mother saw me now, she'd have a second heart attack, I'm sure of it.

"Don't move," he says, and moves toward the whirlpool tub. The water flips on, and I turn toward him, catching sight of his perfect muscled ass as he bends forward, running his hand through the spray and splashing the water onto his face.

I want to say this afternoon with Voss is something I'll never do again as long as I live, and that I should enjoy it while it lasts, but I know that's not true. I've learned a few things about myself in the last half hour.

First, a wine stopper really does feel incredible, even if it's wrong.

And second, I am hopelessly attracted to this man's unapologetic approach to sex. It's evident, the way I haven't moved since he walked away—my arms still bound behind my back, my cheek still flat against the mattress, ass high in the air—that I enjoy his command. His roughness. That I yearn for more of it.

When he turns around to face me again, there's a dark and hungry gleam in his eyes, and I have no doubt this man would eat me alive. Without a word, he slides his hands beneath me and lifts me up into his arms like I weigh nothing.

He sets me down on wobbly legs, and I let him strip away my skirt, then the shirt, like he's systematically peeling away layers of my resistance, until I'm standing completely naked in front of him and yet another mirror above the tub.

It's instinct that draws my hand over my mound, shielding it from his prying eyes, because there's no way in hell I'd have let Denny look at me the way Voss is right now. In fact, I insisted on the lights being turned off during sex.

He pushes my hands away, making a deep masculine sound of appreciation in his chest, and steps into the tub first, flicking his fingers for me to follow. Somehow, he looks bigger in the tub, his body even more imposing than before.

My skin practically sizzles, as I toe the water and step down, letting him draw me onto his lap. Back to his chest, I straddle his legs, as his palm presses against my inner thigh, spreading me open.

Two fingers dip inside me, damn near splitting me in half, and he kisses my shoulder. "'Fraid I'm more than two fingers, *Star Wars*."

Hands to my hips, he guides me onto his fully erect cock, and I have to brace myself when his tip breaches my entrance, far bigger than any other man I've been with.

"I wish I could say I'll be gentle, but you've got me wound so fucking tight right now, I need to get inside you."

Pressing at either side of me, he eases me down, allowing me to stretch around him with tiny thrusts. Inch by inch, he seats himself deeper, tunneling his cock a little more each time. One quick shunt, and I hear him groan behind me, while I remain on my knees, submerged up to my breasts in the water, and back arched, I claw the edge of the tub, letting my body acclimate to the pain of his girth.

"Watching you come with that stopper is the hottest thing I've seen. I need more, but it's my cock that's going to make you shatter like that." He gives another upward thrust and growls in my ear.

"Voss!" I arch further, taking in the fullness of him, while he sits motionless for a moment.

Arms wrap around me, urging me back against him, and he circles his hips, slowly stirring his dick inside of me.

With lazy pumps in and out of me, he pinches my nipples that only just stick up out of the water. "I'm going to take my time with you. The wait is fucking torture, but it's worth it. Tonight is all about you."

"Wait for what?" I curl my fingers and bite my lip, as he drives into me at a maddening deliberate pace.

He doesn't answer, and it doesn't matter, because some-how, *somehow*, he's coaxing my body into arousal again.

I wouldn't think it possible so soon after climax, but the

tightening of my belly, the ache tugging deep inside of me, the hungry monster so starved for this kind of attention it's become insatiable, has awakened once again. Masculine sounds of pleasure vibrate over my skin, as he tugs and toys with my nipples, while his cock stretches and fills me. Powerful, controlled, rocking into me like billowing waves that could easily break into riptides, dragging me under the surface.

For the next hour and a half, he fucks me this way, in the tub, on the bed, keeping me on the edge of climax, until I'm drenched in sweat and every muscle is trembling and fragile.

The man is relentless. His body glistens with all of his toil, but he keeps on like there's some electrical source feeding his cock. I've never known a man to go so long in my life.

I've already climaxed twice while trying to hold out for him. My body is so worn down, my muscles so weak and soft, all I can do is roll my head, as I writhe with his continued assault.

Caged below him, I stare into his eyes, those beautifully unforgiving gray eyes, and reach up to touch his face. "Wait. Please. I need to stop." The hoarse drag of my voice begs for a single drop of water.

Voss finally collapses onto the bed beside me, and removes the flaccid and empty condom from his shaft.

"You didn't …" I can't even say it, the shame of having climaxed twice already heating my cheeks. "How can you … go so *long*?"

"Not easily with you, I'll admit."

"You're saying that was intentional?"

"Today was about you, Nola. Not me." He reaches for the two bottles of water set out on the nightstand and tosses me one.

Cracking the lid, I tip it back, guzzling the ice-cold fluids that damn near sizzle when I swallow, while my mind spins an endless web of questions. Did I do something wrong? Is he turned off? Perhaps thinking of someone else? *Wishing* of someone else?

"Am I …" *A bad lay?* Even Denny came relatively quickly, and that was toward the end when we hated each other.

After one long swig, Voss sets his half-drank water bottle back on the nightstand. "Are you what?"

"I mean … I know I'm a little inexperienced, and all …" I close the cap, running my finger over the top to keep from having to look at him, where he sits sprawled beside me, the embodiment of masculinity. "I've not been with many …"

"You're perfect. Don't question anything about yourself."

"You say that, but that's exactly what I'm doing." Weakly pushing up from the bed, all I want to do is leave and not have to look into those eyes of his again, but the moment I slide from the mattress, I'm yanked back.

Hard.

The mortification ruptures inside of me, and his ridiculous little affirmations are just a slap in the face. "Let me go, Voss."

"Not a chance." Amusement colors his voice, only adding to my frustration, as I muster what little energy is left in me to wriggle away from him, so I can go hide in the bathroom and chide myself for being an idiot. "You're upset about what, exactly? That I didn't want it to be over in a matter of minutes? That I chose to draw it out for as long as I could and savor you?"

"I … um." Feel kind of silly. I didn't think of it that way.

"The pain of anticipation heightens the ecstasy of release. I've built up a lot of stamina, waiting for a woman like you to come along who can take it."

"That's very poetic, Voss. But I don't believe a word of that."

"Whether you believe it, or not, it's true. I could go all night with you, Nola." His still hard cock nudging my ass is a reminder that sends an ache up into my womb. Had I done something wrong, or turned him off, I doubt he'd have kept that monster erect the whole time. "I'd never tire of you." Arm banded across my stomach, he pulls me tighter. "You're the best kind of torture."

"I guess I just feel kind of ... greedy."

"You should feel greedy. You deserve to be greedy. How many assholes would've felt bad for busting a nut inside of you first and calling it a night?"

Too many, unfortunately. I doubt *any* guy I've been with ever bothered to put much thought into my enjoyment.

"Be greedy. Be tenacious with the things that make you feel good. And for fucks sake, don't ever apologize for it."

I want to believe that Voss is everything I've made him up to be in my head—this ridiculously hot alpha who is all about pleasing his female at the expense of his own gratification.

I'm inclined to think he follows his own advice, though, pursuing what he wants unapologetically, so his words don't exactly add up in my head. But regardless, he's right. No man I've ever been with felt bad for using me, so why the hell should I? Particularly if this one is giving me permission to take from him.

And I did. A couple times. It felt pretty damn amazing, too.

Scooting back onto the bed beside him, I curl up into his massive body, wrapping my leg over his hip, where his rock hard erection still sticks up between us. Jesus, the guy must be in agony right now. "I could *try* to get you off, if you wanted."

Palm gripping my thigh, he lifts my leg higher so his tip sits at my entrance. Maybe he's a masochist, or something. "It's okay. You're tired. Get some rest."

He's right. Having gotten up early to prepare for this show, carting all that pottery around, followed by hours of sex, has softened my bones and left me useless. My whole body feels like it's been pummeled, but I can't deny that I didn't enjoy every minute, even the parts that made me a little uncomfortable at first.

"I can't really bear to think of someone using that wine stopper again," I say. "We're just going to toss it, right?"

A chuckle rumbles in his chest. "I had the bellhop pick it up from the gift shop downstairs. It's yours to keep. As a souvenir."

I laugh at that and snuggle into him. "Thank you for this," I whisper, more appreciatively than before.

"What are you thanking me for?"

"For being a decent guy." I yawn and stretch against him, letting his warm body lull me into the afternoon snooze that's calling to me. "Feels like everyone's a psychopath these days."

23

VOSS

A text pops up on my screen, lighting up the dark room as I lay beside Nola. It's only six in the evening, but with the curtains drawn, it feels like the dead of night.

The text is from the company I hired to install cameras on Nola's property, letting me know the project is complete. Every room now has a small, concealed camera that feeds to the app on my phone.

Had Nola gone home three hours ago, she'd have caught them doing the work, and I'd have had to explain shit I wasn't ready to explain yet. To test it, I click on the app, scrolling through the different cameras, until I land on Nola's bedroom. I specifically requested that the camera be added to the Southeast corner of the room, so that I might see anyone passing in the hallway, while keeping a close eye on Nola as she sleeps. I smile, staring down at the empty bed and exit the app.

Beside me, Nola snoozes away, sprawled out and clearly exhausted.

After a half hour of blue balls, my body has finally settled down. I wasn't lying when I said today was about her or that I fully intended to savor every minute. All of this is about her, ultimately. The distraction. The cameras. All with her in mind.

It's not that I'm willing to give at the expense of my own pleasure, because if the conditions were right, I'd have used her body as voraciously as she used mine. I don't like condoms, though, which is why I've historically paid top dollar for clean girls, and I like a bit more fight with my fucking.

Problem is, the role-playing has gotten dull and boring. I've grown tired of girls with rape fantasies, for hire. I want the real deal and I want it with Nola. I could see it in her eyes with the wine stopper, that devilish glint telling me she isn't all sweetness and innocence when it comes to sex.

No, there's something darker living and breathing inside of her, too. Past all that hesitation and inhibition lies what she secretly desires, but will never admit aloud. I see it, though.

She hides it well, but men like me sniff that shit out like dogs on a blood trail.

The woman craves depravity as much as she craves the assurance that no one will ever discover her true nature. For a sadist who's watched her for hours, it's obvious, and her denial is somewhat amusing. Fact is though, Nola would never go for the kind of degrading shit that gets me off. The wine stopper was a good test, but even that took some coaxing, and unfortunately, three hours isn't enough time to erase the lies she's trained herself to believe.

Yet, if she did decide to indulge in some of my darker fantasies, we'd make one hell of a match. The kind that'd burst into flames and set fire to everything around it, because the woman wears sensuality like gasoline perfume.

For the first time in a long time, sex didn't bore the shit

out of me. In truth, watching her come, *hearing* her climax, was everything I've dreamed it would be, but my body craves more from her. It knows what she's capable of, and won't settle for some premature eruption when it could have sweat, claws, and the rush of adrenaline that'd leave me dizzy for her afterward. The kind that'd have me addicted and obsessed. Weak for her.

So maybe it's better I don't indulge. Not yet, anyway.

I run my finger over her cheek, staring down at her angelic face. I've never allowed a woman to sleep in the same bed after sex. Always felt pointless before, particularly as I pay them by the day. But I have to admit, I like being next to her. I like taking care of her, and I particularly like watching her sleep, but it has to come to an end.

Leaning forward, I bury my face in her neck and kiss her there. "Hey, it's after six."

She stretches and yawns against me, and I wrap my arm around her stomach, drawing her into me. "I'm going to call Jonah. See if he'll keep Oli overnight." Rolling over, she hikes her leg over mine and nuzzles against my chest like a little bird.

A little bird I want to cage and keep for myself.

"I mean, you paid for the room, it'd be a waste to leave after three hours."

I snort at that, giving her ass a squeeze. "Make your call, then meet me in the shower."

"Okay."

Hooking a finger beneath her chin, I tip her head back and kiss her, before sliding out of the bed.

As I head toward the bathroom, I hear the appreciative sound she makes before engaging her brother on the other end of the call.

"Jonah? Hey, any chance you can take Oliver overnight? Something ... came up."

I close out the rest of the conversation and flip on the shower. The three hours was an excuse, originally, to kill time. Keep her occupied. Get some much-needed action after a week of playing monk. But I didn't bank on enjoying myself. Sex has always been something of a transaction for me. An exchange of goods. Two weeks ago, Nola was nothing but a warm hole where I might bury my cock at some point, if I got bored, but now she's so much more than that. More than I expected, and I can't quite wrap my head around it.

I never thought past having her. My fantasies were confined to the two of us in bed. Constantly. But never the life around it.

And her life includes variables that I can't add to the equation.

Like a kid.

When this job is over, I'm going back to New York. I'll be swiping criminals up off the streets and torturing them into talking. Not exactly something I'd care to share for Career Day at school.

Nola's young. No doubt, she'll want more kids. She'll want a life and freedom. Things I'll never be able to promise her in my line of work. There's a reason The Gallows is comprised of single and divorced men. Families are a liability, a weakness that can totally fuck up a job.

But I can't let her go now. I've had a taste, and as much as I hoped that would be enough, I already know it's not. She's mouthwatering, like a forbidden fruit I've never had before, but with a pinch of depravity, she'd taste even better.

Steam rolls over the top of the shower, and the door clicks as Nola enters. Arms wrapped around her mid-section, she baffles me. That she would hide a body so perfect, with all her curves and fleshy parts, is beyond me, and as she approaches, I tear her arms away from her, taking a moment to drink her in.

My dick lurches with the visual of her arms strung up over her head, lifting those voluptuous tits where I can suck on them, while she fights to get away.

"When you enter a room, you walk in like you own everything in it. Understand?"

"You're in here. Does that mean I own you, too?"

I don't answer that, because no woman has ever owned me. But Nola? She might just be the exception.

I pull her into the shower stall with me, impatient and more forceful than I intend. That's what she does to me. Every minute I spend with her is precious, like the clock is constantly against me.

24

THE SANDMAN

O*ne week ago …*
Clippers snipped over the dried moonflower seeds that were scattered across a tray The Sandman had set atop a wooden workbench. Sweat trickled down his face from the overhead sunlamps beating over top of him. Though highly poisonous, he sometimes brewed the seeds in tea for the hallucinatory effects, similar to taking LSD. Most enjoyable was sitting in his viewing room, with all the pictures he'd collected, and relieving himself to the visuals of his subjects lying helpless and trapped in their latex binds. It'd often helped during the months when his flowers refused to bloom, which dictated the times he'd go in search of another evening companion.

If consumed in high doses, more than just a few seeds, one would fall into an agitated state, which gradually developed into seizures and hyperthermia, ultimately leading to coma and death.

Witnessing each stage of consumption was as beautiful as observing his Queen of the Night bloom. The excitement of watching life fade from their eyes couldn't be described. The godly power of taking it, claiming it as his own, represented his most ardent fantasy fulfilled.

He dumped the seeds into a jar of water and set them aside.

Vining plants covered up the wall and shelves across from him, in various stages of growth. The prized Queen of the Night in the most spacious pots, among a delicious bone meal and rich compost fertilizer he mixed himself. He'd learned how to encourage blooming in each plant, and kept a steady schedule by constantly repotting and replanting in new pots.

Gathering up the remaining seeds into his palm, he carried them across the room to the bed, where Beth lay entirely incased in clear latex. Only a breathing tube stuck up from the shiny blanket sealed tight to her body.

The Sandman counted the seeds in his hand, making sure there were enough to reach the final stage that time. His last subject, before Marnee, had gotten as far as comatose, before he was forced to extinguish her himself. Twice, he'd missed that glorious bloom of watching their eyes go dull, as he'd been in full-on rapture during Marnee's death.

No, he'd ensure that Beth would consume enough toxic poison that he wouldn't miss it. He'd capture it, save it by removing her eyes and storing them where he could look upon them whenever he wished to relive the moment.

"Beth? Can you hear me?"

She nodded, the panic in her eyes a natural reaction. Some had hyperventilated when he'd completely covered them in plastic that way, but he'd assured Beth that she'd have more than enough air to breathe.

"I'm going to send some seeds down into your breathing tube. I want you to prepare your throat to swallow them. They're completely natural, designed to help you relax. If you remove your mouth from the breathing tube, I'll be forced to take away the tube all together. Am I clear?"

With her emphatic nod, The Sandman smiled.

"Good girl. Now here comes the first couple of seeds. Are you ready?"

Another nod.

Only dumping the first couple into the tube, he watched her swallow them back easily, never once taking her mouth off the tube.

"Very nice. You're very talented at swallowing with something sticking out of your mouth, aren't you?"

Her nervous chuckle vibrated up the breathing tube.

"Now, here are a few more," he said, and dumped a few more down the breathing tube. Only small bits at a time, giving her a chance to swallow after, until his palm sat empty of the seeds. "You're going to feel strange in a while, Beth. You may even begin hallucinating. It's all normal. In the meantime, I'm going to fuck you again. Would you like that?"

Through the plastic, her temples glistened with fallen tears, but she nodded.

"Good, good." If he timed it right, he could work himself up to climax the moment she took her last breath. And what a glorious moment that would be for him.

After removing the dildo he'd placed inside of her, he lined his latex-clad dick with her entrance and pushed himself inside. He was still somewhat flaccid from the hours before, but just staring down at her face through the plastic, with the scent of latex filling his head, was enough to make him hard again.

Nearly an hour passed. Sweat left him feeling sticky against the latex, his cock going from moments of hardness to softness and back again. All the while, she whimpered and whined into the breathing tube, until she finally began to struggle. The breathing tube slipped from her mouth as she shook her head beneath the plastic.

"Let me out! Let me out!" Her muffled voice carried an edge of terror that sent slivers of excitement down his spine. "I want out! I want out of here!"

Ah, panic had settled in, thanks to the seeds.

Latex squeaked and rubbed, as he kept on with fucking her, his stomach knotted with the urge to climax, but he wouldn't.

Her time was coming soon.

He could see the red blush in her cheeks that told him her temperature was elevated.

She hadn't taken the breathing tube back in, which told him she'd gone delirious, perhaps deep in hallucinations. The struggle of her body moving against him was a small distraction, but one he was willing to endure for a few minutes longer.

The struggle ceased.

Only the rapid rise and fall of her chest could be felt beneath him.

He studied her eyes, the way they stared off at nothing in particular. Mouth gaping, the plastic filled the concave space between her lips, where he pressed his own, in a deep and tender kiss, reveling in the bitter taste of latex against his tongue. Fucking her. Kissing her. He lifted his head and peered into her eyes.

He came hard into the cock sheath, the warmth fisting his tip, as he rocked into her with the final spurts.

She stilled.

He would have her one more time just like that, before taking his mementos.

Finally. His most exhilarating experience yet, but it wouldn't hold a candle to what he planned next.

Beth was merely a means to an end. Practice.

He'd find one more subject, to be sure he'd perfected the process, and then he'd move on to his ultimate catch. His *prized* Queen of the Night.

His one true obsession.

Nola Tensley.

———

I hope you enjoyed the first book of the Sandman Duet! Please consider leaving a review. Long or short, your review is always appreciated, and along with telling a friend about the book, it is the most wonderful gift you can give an author 🤍 Thank you for reading.

———

Requiem & Reverie (The Sandman Duet, Book Two) releases on May 13, 2019!
PREORDER NOW

JOIN THE SPOILER & SUPPORT ROOM
and be automatically entered to win a signed paperback set of the duet plus other goodies!

JOIN MY MAILING LIST
for fun giveaways and exclusives

Chapter 1
Voss

"I want to show you something," Carl says. Shadows slice across his face, where he stands alongside my bed. "C'mon."

The room is dark, and the tone of his voice carries an unsettling edge of amusement that makes me reluctant to do as he says. I follow after him, anyway, even though Grandfather would be furious to know I've gotten out of bed, because it's the lesser of two evils. If I don't, Carl will take pleasure in tormenting me tomorrow.

We pad down the hallway to the door that leads to the cellar. I never understood why it was located at the end of this particular corridor, when the house holds so many rooms and hallways between the north and south wing. It's no secret grandfather chooses to keep Carl and me as far away from him as possible, and perhaps this hallway is merely a step up from making us sleep in the cellar itself.

Whispers reach my ear, as I approach the dark door that's crafted of thick ornate wood. At night, without the hallway lights on, it looks like a vacuous hole that would pull an unsus-pecting passerby in and swallow him up.

A faint voice reaches my ears, like a cold breeze across my skin, springing goosebumps. "Don't let him hurt me."

Carl opens the door to the cellar, his face still obscured by the darkness, which hides the smile I know is there as he moves aside to let me pass.

With careful steps, I descend the stairs. and the whispers seem to get louder. Or maybe the surrounding emptiness just becomes more pronounced the farther I go, like walking into a tomb.

I follow the sound to a room with empty shelves, where grandfather once kept all his tools and supplies. The place I first watched Carl slice open a baby mouse he found, while it was still alive.

Little light penetrates this room, but I can make out a figure lying on the floor. A girl.

Seems no more than a blink later, and Carl is lying on top of her, driving his hips into her, but his eyes are on me. The wicked grin stretched across his face is a trigger that incites my nerves, urging me to attack. He wraps his hands around her throat, and as I approach, her face slowly comes into view.

Nola.

My blood turns hot, every muscle taut with the anger pumping through my veins. I rush toward him, knocking him off of her, and wrap my arms around his throat.

"She's mine! Fucking mine!" Digging my fingers into his gullet, I tell myself to end it. Kill him now. How long I've fanta-sized about the moment when I can watch life drain from his body.

"Voss!" he chokes out. "Please!"

His pleas only goad me to press harder, to squeeze every last ounce of breath out of him.

"Voss!" It's not Carl's voice, but Nola's.

The face below me morphs into hers, and the moment I release her throat, her body turns limp. Her head falls to the side, eyes vacant and dull.

A tremble starts deep inside of me and ripples into waves of agony, as I stare down at my hands. My murdering hands.

Requiem & Reverie (The Sandman Duet, Book Two) releases on May 13, 2019

PREORDER

OTHER BOOKS BY KERI LAKE

CONTEMPORARY ROMANCE

RICOCHET

BACKFIRE

INTREPID

BALLISTIC

EROTIC ROMANCE

RIPPLE EFFECT

PARANORMAL ROMANCE

SOUL AVENGED

SOUL RESURRECTED

SOUL ENSLAVED

SOUL REDEEMED

THE FALLEN (A SONS OF WRATH SPINOFF)

DYSTOPIAN ROMANCE

JUNIPER UNRAVELING

Sign up to Keri's newsletter for a chance to win ARCs of upcoming
releases!

ABOUT THE AUTHOR

Keri Lake is a dark romance writer who specializes in demon wrangling, vengeance dealing and wicked twists. Her stories are gritty, with antiheroes that walk the line of good and bad, and feisty heroines who bring them to their knees. When not penning books, she enjoys spending time with her husband, daughters, and their rebellious Labrador (who doesn't retrieve a damn thing). She runs on strong coffee and alternative music, loves a good red wine, and has a slight addiction to dark chocolate.

Keep up with Keri's new releases and get free books:
VIP EMAIL SIGN UP

Join Keri's reading group for giveaways, fun chats and a chance to win advance copies of her books:
VIGILANTE VIXENS

She loves hearing from readers …
www.KeriLake.com